Zufar's chest filled with grim purpose as his gaze swung from the unsuitable woman before him to the wedding dress and back again.

"Come here," he commanded evenly.

The chambermaid jerked into movement, advancing to a stop two feet away from him.

He inspected her, noting her eyes held gold flecks within the chocolate depths. His gaze dropped, took in the lines of her neck, and again he experienced a tiny bolt of surprise at how sleekly it curved to her shoulders, how delicate and flawless she was.

Decision made, he whirled away from her. As if his aides were in tune with his thoughts, a brief knock sounded on the door before they rushed in.

"Your Highness? Have you any news you wish me to relay to the royal guard?"

"My marriage ceremony is still going ahead." He slashed his hand through the shocked murmurs. When he achieved silence, he continued. "I fully intend to be married in two hours' time. Neisha Zalwani is to be my bride, and everyone in this room will ensure that my wishes are fulfilled."

Bound to the Desert King

One scandalous royal family, four irresistible sheikhs!

The royal family of Khalia has always presented an image of duty and responsibility. But the brother they never knew existed has just stepped into the palace—and soon all their lives will change forever!

Adir was exiled to the desert, then brutally rejected—now he's back for vengeance!

Sheikh's Baby of Revenge by Tara Pammi

Zufar's bride of convenience has just been kidnapped—now the maid must take her place...

Sheikh's Pregnant Cinderella by Maya Blake

Available now!

Galila has just told her family's secrets to a stranger—but he's king of a neighboring kingdom!

Sheikh's Princess of Convenience by Dani Collins

Malak is now heir to the throne—but a secret in his past is about to be uncovered...

Sheikh's Secret Love-Child by Caitlin Crews

Coming soon!

Maya Blake

—

SHEIKH'S PREGNANT CINDERELLA

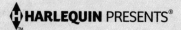

Recycling programs for this product may not exist in your area.

Special thanks and acknowledgment are given to Maya Blake for her contribution to the Bound to the Desert King miniseries.

ISBN-13: 978-1-335-41967-5

Sheikh's Pregnant Cinderella

First North American publication 2018

Copyright © 2018 by Harlequin Books S.A.

HARLEQUIN®
www.Harlequin.com

Printed in U.S.A.

Maya Blake's hopes of becoming a writer were born when she picked up her first romance at thirteen. Little did she know her dream would come true! Does she still pinch herself every now and then to make sure it's not a dream? Yes, she does! Feel free to pinch her, too, via Twitter, Facebook or Goodreads! Happy reading!

Books by Maya Blake

Harlequin Presents

A Diamond Deal with the Greek
Signed Over to Santino
Pregnant at Acosta's Demand
The Sultan Demands His Heir
His Mistress by Blackmail

One Night With Consequences

The Boss's Nine-Month Negotiation

Secret Heirs of Billionaires

Brunetti's Secret Son

Rival Brothers

A Deal with Alejandro
One Night with Gael

Visit the Author Profile page
at Harlequin.com for more titles.

CHAPTER ONE

HIS EARS WERE playing tricks on him. They must be.

Otherwise they wouldn't have relayed the unconscionable message to his brain that—

No.

'Repeat yourself,' Sheikh Zufar al Khalia, current occupant of the throne of Khalia, breathed softly at the short, bespectacled senior aide standing before him.

The man shrank back, very much aware that his King's lowered, even tones were far worse than his bark. Not that Zufar al Khalia, much accomplished, master strategist and all-round frighteningly intelligent head of the exulted royal family, needed to lower himself to such unseemly actions as barking.

Marwan Farhat only managed to withstand his liege's chilling tawny gaze for a handful of seconds before lowering his to the priceless Persian rug beneath his feet.

'Now, Marwan,' Zufar insisted.

'We've been informed that your betrothed has disappeared, Your Highness. She's not in her suite, and her maidservant thinks she's been taken.'

'Thinks? So there's no actual evidence?'

'Uh... I haven't spoken to the servant myself, Your Highness, but—'

'For all you know, my betrothed could be hiding somewhere in the palace, under the pretext of the foolish, pre-wedding nerves that normally afflict women on such a day, correct?'

Marwan exchanged glances with the other aides. 'It is possible, Your Highness.'

Zufar heard the *but* not spoken, loud and clear. 'Where is this maidservant? I wish to speak to her myself.'

The senior aide grimaced. 'Of course, Your Highness, but I've been informed the girl is quite hysterical. I don't think it will be useful—'

'Useful?' The cold disbelief trapped in his chest expanded. 'Do you see what I'm wearing, Marwan?' Zufar drawled in the soft, deadly voice that usually hushed his subordinates into fearful silence, as he rounded the massive teak desk that had previously belonged to his esteemed grandfather.

Marwan's Adam's apple bobbed again as he took in Zufar's heavy burgundy-and-gold military uniform, complete with wide sash, epaulettes, and buttons made of solid gold. Where other men would have looked stiff and pompous, his King looked enviably elegant, his towering six-feet-plus height lending the uniform a regal stature few could emulate.

The accompanying cloak hung on its own specially made frame nearby. Together they formed the King's ceremonial wedding attire, commissioned on his twenty-first birthday for this one momentous occasion. Zufar al Khalia had cut a commanding figure since he hit puberty, but on this day he rose above all men into an exclusive realm of his own.

'Yes, Your Highness,' he responded respectfully.

Zufar tossed the white gloves he'd been about to put on before he was interrupted onto the desk, and advanced towards the men. He had their attention, but he needed to make sure that not a single syllable that fell from his lips would be misconstrued.

'Have you seen the dignitaries and heads of states currently making their way to the Imperial Room? The fifty thousand citizens who've been camping in the capital for the past seven days in anticipation of this ceremony? The three hundred journalists and innumerable cameras waiting on the south lawn to televise this ceremony?'

'Of course, Your Highness.'

Zufar took a deep calming breath, certain that if he didn't he would burst a blood vessel despite his supremely robust health. And that would be terribly unwise considering this was supposed to be his wedding day.

'Tell me again why you think it would not be *useful* to discover the whereabouts of my betrothed as soon as possible?'

Marwan clasped his hands before him, a gesture of supplication that did nothing to appease Zufar's rising temper. 'A thousand pardons, Your Highness,' he said. 'I merely came to inform you that there might be a delay. Perhaps we can postpone the ceremony—'

'No. There will be no postponement. You will find my betrothed immediately and this wedding ceremony will proceed as scheduled.'

'Your Highness, the guards and all the servants have searched everywhere. She is not here.'

A red haze washed across Zufar's vision. His collar began to constrict him, blocking his airway. But he didn't raise his hand to undo a button or in any way indicate his discomfort.

He was the King.

Since birth, streams of instructors and governesses had drummed long-suffering poise and decorum into him, with swift and merciless punishment delivered for stepping out of line. As for rash displays of emotion like the bellow of frustration that bubbled inside him? Those came with a week's banishment to the winter palace on the northernmost part of Khalia with nothing but the frozen mountains and endless reams of Latin recitals for company.

No, unfettered displays of emotion had been his father's eminent domain.

For Zufar and his younger brother and sister, it had been an emotionless existence in the strictest boarding schools in foreign lands. And during the holidays when they were allowed home, they would spend hours being groomed into becoming the perfect ambassadors of the Royal House of Khalia.

On the rare occasion when his temper strained and attempted to get the better of him, like today, people took notice. And fled his presence at the earliest possible moment.

Zufar gathered himself until his spine was a steel column, and fixed his eyes on Marwan. 'You will take me to this maidservant now. I wish to hear what she has to say for myself.'

The senior aide immediately bowed low. 'Of course, Your Highness.'

The palace guards stationed on either side of the door sprang forwards to open the double doors for him.

The moment Zufar stepped into the hallway, he knew

something was very, very wrong. The excited buzz that had charged the air during the final preparations for the royal wedding had altered.

Several staff members of the royal palace wore anxious expressions as they rushed back and forth. And while it was respectful to drop one's gaze before the King, he noticed that every single one of the staff was actively avoiding his.

The palpable tension raised the hairs on his nape. Beside him, Marwan also avoided his gaze. In fact, the man was doing everything in his power to extend his short strides in the rush to put self-preserving space between himself and Zufar.

It would've been amusing had Zufar not felt in his very marrow that his impending nuptials were in jeopardy.

Whispers around him grew as he entered the main part of the palace. As with most royal palaces, the women's quarters were separated from the men's by several wings. His own private rooms were to the west of the sprawling palace that sat on top of Mount Jerra.

Quick strides took him across to the east wing. He ignored the bows and scrapes of his palace staff and extended family members as he walked, grim-faced, towards the guest suite that Amira, his fiancée, had occupied since her arrival at the palace three weeks ago.

She was a daughter of his father's oldest friend, and Zufar had been aware of Amira's existence since he was a boy. But she was several years his junior and had clearly found him intimidating to the point of speechlessness at the best of times. He hadn't taken much interest in her until his father had informed him of the agreement he'd made with Feroz Ghalib, Amira's father, for them to marry.

Even then, the wedding had been a distant future event, arranged by others and needing only a handful of meetings for the sake of appearances. Still, he'd taken his duty seriously and ensured during their meetings that she was at ease and not being forced into a union she didn't want. Her assurances had satisfied him enough to accept that she would be his wife when the time was right.

The medical report that had confirmed that she was healthy enough to bear his children had sealed the deal.

Beyond that, he hadn't given her much thought, although she'd been peculiarly distracted during their twice weekly dinners recently.

But Amira was close with his sister and Zufar was confident that Galila would have informed him if there'd been a problem with the upcoming nuptials.

Nevertheless, had he dropped the ball somewhere?

He frowned.

The burden of governing his kingdom was his first and only priority. It had needed to be, considering the chaos it had been left in by his father's sudden abdication.

Tight anger knotted inside him as he strode faster towards the suite of luxury rooms that were reserved for the Queen and other female members of the royal family.

He wouldn't think of his father today, or the fact that the ex-King had banished himself to the summer palace since his wife's death and hadn't spoken to his children in months. Zufar wouldn't think of the sleepless nights and backbreaking work it had taken for him to keep the kingdom that had already been woefully neglected by his father from falling apart.

Today, *this hour*, demanded his complete attention. His people yearned for a royal wedding. That was exactly what he was going to give them.

The footmen stationed outside the Sapphire Suite spotted him and immediately threw open the doors.

Zufar entered, then drew to a stop at the sight of the visibly distressed women in the living room. Two were babbling hysterically, and an older female servant was busy comforting another.

'Which one is she?' he demanded tersely. Eyes swivelled to him, followed predictably by shocked gasps and hurried comportment before the bows and scrapes and averted gazes commenced.

Marwan hushed them, and then uttered a sharp query to the junior aide behind him. The younger man shook his head, throwing a furtive glance at Zufar. Marwan approached the older attendant and questioned her. Clearly nervous, she pointed to the inner chamber.

Zufar strode towards smaller double doors, his temper frothing furiously in his chest. This time he pulled the doors open himself, bitter memories tossing themselves onto the pyre he was trying to contain as he walked into the huge, lavish chamber that had once been his mother's domain.

His gaze didn't linger on the priceless keepsakes, furniture or decoration. He didn't know which items in this room his mother had treasured and which gifts from his father and her secret admirers had been less favoured. He didn't know her favourite book or the preferred flower arrangement for her private sitting room because he had never been allowed in here.

On the rare occasions his mother had tolerated him, they had been in public where her pretended adoration could be captured for the world to see and praise and to provide moments of smugness as she perused the gossip rags. Beyond that, she'd never had a kind word for him or his siblings.

But he wasn't here to dwell on the subject of his mother.

He trained his focus on the figure hunched over near the headboard of the vast bed. She was so slight he almost missed her.

Had it not been for the drab, body-shrouding beige clothes that painfully and distastefully stood out against the gold and cream bed linen, he would've mistaken her for one of the pillows or part of the rich drapery that decorated the four-poster bed.

As he advanced towards her he noticed that her slim shoulders were shaking. Another few steps and the small sniffles of her quiet sobs reached his ears.

Zufar stifled his curse before it ripped free.

He didn't care for weak women. He cared even less for weak, *crying* women.

Behind him, Marwan clicked his tongue sharply.

The figure jumped up, stumbled over her long, shapeless skirt, and immediately tumbled to the floor in a graceless heap at Zufar's feet.

He waited, impatient breath slowly spilling through clenched teeth, for her to rise. But she didn't seem interested in regaining her feet. Instead, she was developing an almost mesmerised interest in his shoes.

He took a step forwards, hoping to dislodge her hypnosis. When that failed to work, he cleared his throat.

'If that is a shoe fetish you're exhibiting, may I suggest you indulge in it another time? When the reputation of my kingdom isn't at stake, perhaps?' Zufar drawled.

A sharp intake of breath, then, finally, she raised her head.

Large, tear-soaked dark eyes rose from his feet, and plotted an excruciatingly slow journey up his body. By the time they reached his face, her expression was creased into abject horror.

Coupled with a face blotched and bloated with tears and a mouth frozen in an unattractive O, she was the most unsightly girl Zufar had ever seen.

'What is your name?' he bit out, praying she could actually string enough words together to answer.

She didn't respond. She simply stared up at him, her horror intensifying by the second.

'Do you not hear your King addressing you, girl?' Marwan demanded sharply.

Her mouth closed. She swallowed noisily, but still uttered no word.

Zufar's fists started to curl. Almost a year's worth of meticulous planning hung in the balance because of one tear-streaked, dumbstruck girl.

About to move, he paused as her gaze darted to his fists and she recoiled.

The sight of her naked fear struck an uncomfortable chord in him. He breathed out and slowly unfurled his fingers. There would be no coherent conversation with her unless he found a way to defuse some of her fear, he realised.

He sensed Marwan moving towards her and held up his hand. 'Leave us,' he instructed.

Marwan made a small sound of surprise. 'Are you sure, Your Highness?'

Zufar's lips tightened. 'Leave. Now.'

The room emptied immediately. He kept his gaze fixed on the girl crouched before him, and slowly extended his hand towards her. Again, her gaze darted between his face and his hand, as if terrified he would do something unpredictable. Like bite. Or strike.

He frowned.

She reminded him of the skittish colts in his stable. The ones that demanded substantial time and patience to respond to his commands.

Except he was in gross negative supply of either today. His marriage ceremony was scheduled to commence in less than two hours.

Zufar leaned down and extended his hand further. 'Stand up,' he instructed, firming his voice.

She placed her hand in his, scrambled upright, and immediately gasped and dropped his hand as if she'd been scalded.

He ignored her reaction, his gaze moving over her, confirming that the drabness indeed extended from the top of the dishevelled tufts of dark hair peeking out of her beige scarf to the soles of her feet.

Except, she wasn't a girl as he'd initially surmised.

She was long past adolescence, if the pronounced swell of her chest and the hint of curves beneath the clothes were any indication. She came up to his chin in her flat, tasteless shoes, her covered arms slender and her jaw holding a delicate strength.

His eyes were drawn to her chest again. It was just her agitated breathing that was snagging his attention. Nothing else. He stepped back, folded his hands behind his back and assumed a gesture of ease that never failed to work on his horses.

'What is your name?' he asked again in a lower voice.

Her gaze dropped to the ground and she mumbled.

'Speak up,' he said.

Her chin jerked up a little, but her gaze remained, once again, on the tips of his shoes.

'Niesha Zalwani, Your Highness,' she repeated.

Her voice was soft, smoky and lyrical, if a little too timid for his dwindling patience. But at least he was getting somewhere. He had a name.

'What is your role here?'

'I—I'm… I was a chambermaid until last week, when I was added to Miss Amira's personal staff.'

'Look at me when I'm addressing you,' Zufar drawled. It took an interminable age for her head to rise once more. But eventually, her gaze met his, then promptly flitted down to rest on his nose. Zufar prayed for strength and continued, 'Where's your mistress?'

Immediately her lower lip wobbled, her wide eyes grew haunted and her breathing turned agitated again. Zufar forced himself not to stare at the soft globes of her breasts or the pale creaminess of her throat as she trembled before him.

'She…she's gone, Your Highness.'

Zufar's fist threatened to ball again. Resisting the urge was difficult. 'Gone where?' he managed through clenched teeth.

'I don't know, Your Highness.'

'Very well. Let us try another way. Did she leave alone?'

Another frenzied twisting of her fingers, and then she cleared her throat. 'No, Your Highness. She…she left with a man.'

A detached, icy sensation stroked his nape. 'A man? What man?' he asked softly.

'He did not tell me his name, Your Highness.'

'But you are certain she has been taken against her will by an unknown male?' he pressed.

The woman before him bit her lip, drawing his attention to the plump, reddened curve of her mouth as she nodded. 'Yes…well…' Her distress grew.

'Tell me what you know,' he insisted.

'I may be wrong, Your Highness, but she didn't seem…unwilling.'

The possibility that he'd been jilted arrived with ice-cold anger. Except, curiously, Zufar wasn't enraged on his own behalf. Rather, the impending disappointment for his people, the chaos for his kingdom, was what caused his fists to clench behind his back.

'Did she say anything? Did *he* say anything to make you think this?'

'It—it all happened very quickly, Your Highness. But…' Her hand disappeared into the folds of her skirt and emerged with a folded piece of paper. 'He…he instructed me to give this to Princess Galila to hand to you.' She held out the piece of paper, her slender fingers trembling.

Zufar took it from her, his insides frozen as he unfolded the sheet he recognised as a torn piece of his own royal stationery.

He read the message once. Then again.

With a thick curse, he crumpled the heavy, embossed paper between his fingers, his fist clenched tight until it shook with the force of his emotions. The red haze of fury returned, deeper, steeping his lethal mood as he crossed to the window and pressed his fist against the wide pane.

Before him, the palace grounds sprawled in sun-dappled splendour. Beyond the windows, the muted buzzing of an expectant crowd rolled over the horizon. Excited citizens and eager tourists who'd flown in especially for this occasion were anticipating a fairy-tale royal wedding of their King to his chosen Queen. The whole kingdom had been gripped in wedding fever for months.

Only to have his heathen bastard of a half-brother claim in writing that he'd seduced and stolen his betrothed!

In another life, perhaps, that tiny sliver of emotion piercing through his fury could've been called relief from yet another responsibility. But Zufar gave it absolutely no room whatsoever, because he now faced a monumental problem. Aside from the humiliation of announcing that he was no longer in possession of his fiancée, this arrangement had held great economic advantages for Khalia.

He needed to find Amira. Confirm for himself that his half-brother's claim was the truth.

But how could he, when he had no idea where he'd gone? The dossier he'd collated on Adir when he'd first made his unforgettable appearance at his mother's funeral had revealed he had no fixed abode, or, if he did, he'd kept it very well hidden.

Even if Zufar knew his whereabouts, he had no time to go chasing after him. He acknowledged with a bitter laugh how well timed Adir's revenge had been. His half-brother knew that doing this now would cause the most humiliation. The most uproar.

Zufar wasn't about to hand him that victory. Not in this lifetime.

He whirled to face the young chambermaid. 'When did they leave?'

Her throat worked again. But this time she wasn't silent for very long. 'I brought her tea, and left her alone for just ten minutes.' Her voice was wracked with nerves and anguish. She began to wring her hands again. 'I had gone to get the royal jewellery when I heard the commotion.'

'So you saw them leave together?'

Her head moved in a shaky nod. 'Yes.'

'And you're sure he didn't harm her?' Zufar demanded.

'She—she didn't appear in distress, Your Highness. She seemed…willing.'

The tightness in his chest eased a tiny fraction. 'How did they leave?'

She pointed to the very window where he stood.

Zufar's jaw clenched tight. They were on the second floor, with nothing outside the windows but climbing vines. Granted, they were over a century old and sturdy enough to hold a horse, but had his barbarian brother really whisked his betrothed out of a second-floor window?

'Did anyone else see them?'

'Only Her Highness, the Princess, but they were almost on the ground when she came in.'

Zufar frowned. Why hadn't Galila informed him?

Had she tried to stop them and been unsuccessful? Most likely Galila was keeping well out of Zufar's way because she knew how he would take the news.

'How soon after did you raise the alarm?'

Guilt flickered across her face and her lower lip trembled once more.

'Seconds? Minutes?' he snapped.

She paled. 'I—I'm sorry… I thought… I thought it was a prank.'

'It wasn't. And your failure to raise the alarm in time may have aided his getaway.' Zufar was sure of it.

She shrank further into the wall. He whirled away, tension threatening to break his spine.

The scandal just waiting to be triggered by such a revelation struck him stone cold. But under no circumstances was he going to let that happen.

He shoved the piece of paper into his pocket and closed his mind to the burning gross insult against his kingdom and his crown. He would deal with his half-brother later. For now he needed an interim solution to this situation. One that did not involve calling off his wedding.

A quick glance around the room showed the suspended state of preparation.

The gown that should've been adorning his bride-to-be by was draped over a mannequin, the heeled slippers peeking out beneath its hem.

Detachedly, he inspected the rest of the room as he mentally ran through the list of other bridal candidates that had been presented to him when the subject of his nuptials first came up a year ago. Like most royal arranged marriages, although one choice had been favoured above the others, there were always contingencies in case of sudden unsuitability.

Three of those candidates were downstairs, ruled out as potential brides to the King and reduced to honoured guests at his wedding. Could one of them be elevated to the position that would turn out to be a dream come true for them?

Zufar's lips twisted.

There was no way to execute that plan without announcing to the whole world that he'd been jilted. That would only result in frenzied tabloid gossip the media would feed off for years.

Not that any solution he came up with wouldn't cause ripples. But keeping it under wraps until *he* was ready would control the beast.

Which meant he had to keep the circle of trust as tight as possible while he found a quieter, interim solution.

But to mitigate the uproar of impending scandal, he needed a bride; needed to ensure he was married within the next two hours before news that he'd been jilted got out.

His reason for choosing his new bride would need to be explained, of course. That would be a problem for tomorrow.

He turned away from the wedding gown and came face to face with the chambermaid. He'd forgotten about her. To be honest, she was barely breathing, striving to be as unobtrusive as possible. Zufar was surprised she hadn't fled while his back was turned.

Her wide-eyed gaze fixed on him, watchful and wary as she followed his pacing figure.

He slowed to a stop on the next pass, an impossibly ludicrous idea taking root in his brain. 'How long have you been in my palace?' he asked.

'All...um... Most of my life, Y-Your Highness,' she stammered.

He gave a satisfied inner nod. She would know his customs, know the value of discretion.

Sweet desert stars, was he really entertaining this preposterous notion? 'And how old are you?' Zufar growled.

She swallowed, her nostrils quivering delicately as she inhaled. 'Twenty-five, Your Highness.'

He stared at her for a full minute, then nodded briskly. There was neither chagrin nor prevarication in the decision his brain latched onto.

He needed a solution, and he'd found one. His gaze dropped down to her twisting ringless fingers. 'Do you have a husband?' he asked.

A deep blush flamed her cheeks, her gaze flitting away from his again as she shook her head. 'No, Your Highness, I am unmarried.'

Just to be sure, he probed deeper. 'Are you committed to another?'

Her mouth tightened for the briefest second, but she shook her head before she mumbled, 'No.'

He wanted to demand that she repeat that. To look him in the eyes while she did so. But time was slipping through his fingers.

Zufar's chest filled with grim purpose as his gaze sprang from the unsuitable woman before him to the wedding dress, and back again. She was roughly the same size as Amira, if perhaps a little bustier and wider of hip than his...*former* fiancée. Their heights too were similar and so, from what he could see beneath the blotchiness and drabness, was their colouring.

Of course, Amira had held herself with more poise than this maid, years of first-class schooling and a finishing school in Switzerland undertaken for the sole purpose of her future role as Queen. The woman in front of him was nowhere near as polished.

But he didn't need a gem, just a polished stone to pass off as the real thing until he could resolve this situation quietly and on his terms.

'Come here,' he commanded evenly as he strolled to stand next to the wedding dress. Now he'd decided what to do, he couldn't afford any more tears or, heaven forbid, tantrums that would further delay him.

She presented him with that rabbit-caught-in-headlights look again, the pulse fluttering at her throat racing faster.

Zufar bit down his exasperation. 'You're not deaf. I know you can hear me. Come here,' he stated firmly.

She jerked into movement, stumbling to a stop two feet away from him.

He inspected her, noting that her eyes were in fact a dark amethyst, not the brown he'd thought, and that her eyelashes were far longer than he had initially noticed. Her mouth too was curved in a perfect little bow that, should it ever find its way into a smile, might salvage some of her dreariness.

His gaze dropped, took in the lines of her neck, and again experienced a tiny bolt of surprise at how sleekly it curved to her shoulders, how delicate and flawless were her collarbones and skin.

No, not a diamond, but perhaps a better quality stone than he'd first surmised.

A quality stone, but still rough around the edges, he modified, when he noticed she was still twisting her fingers into an agitated mess. 'Be still, little one,' he commanded.

She made a strangled little sound under her breath but her body stilled and her fingers stopped moving. He suppressed a need to tell her to straighten her spine and look him in the eye when he spoke to her.

Such training was unnecessary for what he had in mind. All that would be required was for her not to collapse into a useless heap before he'd achieved his goal. And he had a way to ensure that happened.

Decision made, he whirled away from her. As if they were in tune with his thoughts, a brief knock sounded on the door before Marwan and the rest of his aides rushed in.

'Your Highness? Have you any news you wish me to relay to the royal guard? A starting point for the search for your intended, perhaps?'

'We are past that, Marwan,' Zufar said coldly, noting absently again that Amira's absconding didn't sting as much as it should. If anything, it was his half-brother's insult that grated harsher.

'Oh? Does that mean the ceremony is off?'

Zufar glanced at the woman standing shell-shocked in the corner of the room.

She looked even worse, as if a fresh bolt of lightning had hit her. His decision didn't waver as his gaze objectively raked her.

The wedding bouquet would occupy her skittish hands, veils would shroud her face, and heels would elevate her height and hopefully correct her posture.

Beyond that, very little mattered.

'No, it does not. The ceremony is still going ahead.' He slashed his hand through the shocked murmurs echoing through the room. When he achieved silence, he continued, 'I fully intend to be married in two hours' time. Niesha Zalwani is to be my bride and everyone in this room will ensure that my wishes are fulfilled.'

CHAPTER TWO

'TELL YOUR BROTHER I've not only seduced his precious bride but that she runs away with me willingly. Tell him I'm stealing away his future Queen, just as he stole my birthright.'

Those were the most scandalous words Niesha had expected to hear today, and possibly for the rest of her days. A day that should've been one of intense joy, but which had taken a wrong turn to hell about an hour ago.

With the Sheikh's appearance in his intended's bedroom, she'd harboured hope that everything would be resolved.

Except King Zufar al Khalia had just spoken words that simply didn't make sense. For a moment Niesha wondered whether the shock of watching Amira Ghalib disappear from right under her nose had dislodged a few million brain cells.

The man in front of her, the formidable, extraordinarily captivating tower of masculinity who prowled through his kingdom with harsh authority and power, commanding and receiving the loyal adulation of his subjects because he was simply that breathtaking, had just said—

No. You did you not hear him right. It was impossible.

Her thoughts were clearly echoed by Marwan, who sprang forwards. 'Your Highness?' His voice was ashen with disbelief.

The King—*her* King, since she too was a subject of the Kingdom of Khalia—moved another step closer, bringing his earth-shaking life force even more dangerously into her space. He stalked so close she could almost see the ice crackling in his eyes, the contained fury vibrating his body.

Niesha shrank away from the elegant folds of the wedding gown, the sheets of icy shock thawing into a cauldron of panic. She glanced around the room, selfishly wishing Princess Galila were still here.

King Zufar's sister barely noticed Niesha most of the time, but her kind smile when she did was far better than the fiercely domineering glower of her brother, and the tableau of horrified expressions spread in panorama before her.

Perversely, those expressions were what hammered home the fact that she'd heard correctly. He'd used her full name. In connection to marriage. *His* marriage. Today. Shock gurgled in her throat.

Her fingers moved then, connected with the soft, warm folds of the most extraordinary wedding gown she'd ever seen in her life. The gown that, finding herself alone in this room three nights ago, she'd secretly indulged in one insane moment's fantasy of wearing herself to marry the ephemeral man of her dreams.

The gown that Zufar al Khalia wanted her to…to—

'I'm sorry, Your Highness…' she whispered, but his voice overrode hers.

'Time is of the essence,' he growled, without raising his deep voice. 'I suggest we begin preparations immediately.'

'Your Highness, this…this will be highly unprecedented,' Marwan said.

'I should hope so, or there would be something seriously disturbing with my reign,' Sheikh Zufar stated without looking the old man's way. 'But make no mistake. This wedding ceremony will happen. She is the one who will take Amira's place,' he uttered with a finality that drove a bolt of fear down Niesha's throat.

Aware that she had to get herself together very quickly or risk being flattened by the force of nature bearing down on her, she straightened her spine and raised her head.

He was watching her with the savage, mesmerising golden eyes of a hawk. Before she could summon any words, Marwan beat her to it. 'Your Highness, perhaps we should discuss this—'

'You are risking insubordination by questioning my command. The subject isn't up for discussion. Get the bridal attendants in here now.'

Niesha realised her head was moving from side to side, a pendulous action she couldn't stop. Shockwaves that hadn't stopped rippling through her since she witnessed Amira and the stranger's extraordinary flight now threatened to drown her. Another sound ripped from her throat.

Dark, tawny eyes zeroed in on her.

'You will not pass out,' Zufar commanded tersely, as if just by issuing the edict, her body would follow. 'Bring her a glass of water,' he tossed over his shoulder.

A cut-crystal glass instantly appeared.

With elegant fingers and an unwavering gaze, he handed it to her.

Niesha took a sip, swallowed it along with the hysterical laughter bubbling up. This wasn't happening. She wanted to go back to an hour ago, when she was the least significant person in the room, no different from the straggly orphan without a past she'd been some twenty odd years ago, the one who'd been absorbed by the state orphanage that bore the royal family's name.

The hand-me-down clothes she wore were two sizes too large, and really should have done their job of hiding her better, she mused dazedly. She'd chosen them out of prudence, not fashion. It had simply meant she wouldn't have to worry about new clothes any time soon.

Except, even covered from head to toe, she felt more naked now than she'd ever felt in her life.

'Drink some more,' he decreed.

Her hands shook wildly, but she managed to take another sip without spilling it. He promptly relieved her of the glass. Still dazed, Niesha watched as it was spirited away.

Then her eyes clashed with his, and the words he'd spoken rose like a horrifying mirage before her eyes. Beyond the space filled out by his broad shoulders and his overwhelming presence, Niesha spotted movement as the bridal attendants entered.

He flicked a wrist, and Halimah, the head attendant of the women's wing, who'd barely tolerated Niesha before today, approached.

Zufar acknowledged her presence with a single glance. 'I do not take your loyalty for granted. But I demand your discretion in this matter.'

'Of course, Your Highness,' Halimah replied.

Zufar nodded. 'My new bride has been selected. You

will ensure Niesha is ready at the allotted time. Is that clear?'

Halimah's eyes widened as she stared up at her King.

'Is there a problem?' he demanded.

Her head lowered immediately. 'No, Your Highness.'

Another tremble swept through Niesha as he continued, 'You will dress her and present her to the Grand Hall ready for her royal parade in one hour.' The deep, dark, ruthless timbre of his voice brooked no argument.

No. This wasn't happening.

She was just a maidservant. An orphan with no past. A nobody. She wasn't even worthy of wearing Amira's cast-offs, never mind her wedding gown!

'Please,' she started. The word emerged as a weak, scratchy sound. She cleared her throat and tried again. 'Your Highness, I beg your pardon, but I cannot.'

Pure thunder rumbled across his impressive eyebrows. His eyes, so direct, so hypnotic, drilled right into her bone marrow.

'Yes, you will. Unless you prefer to suffer the consequences of disobeying your King you will go forwards with this.'

Niesha balled her hand and placed it over her racing heart, desperate to calm it before it burst out of her chest. A long time ago, she'd sworn allegiance to him and his family. It had been one of the conditions of inhabiting the palace, and she'd done so willingly. And although he had no inkling who she was or her very small insignificant role his life, she'd done everything asked of her, for him.

In her own way, she'd given him moments of comfort, she liked to tell herself, by making sure that the food she was tasked to serve him in his private dining room was the right temperature, by ensuring his favourite wines were on hand when he returned to his royal apartments after long days away from the palace.

On one occasion, she'd taken it upon herself to purchase a bottle out of her meagre savings when the palace delivery had been delayed.

And when his personal cleaning staff had come down with the flu, she'd volunteered to work in his private quarters. To this day, tucked away in her mind, Niesha had a memory of the scent of his sheets and the unique cologne he wore on his skin.

Those tiny, insignificant but intense moments had made her blush for weeks afterwards on recollection. Still made her blush.

So, yes, like everyone else in this room, she would do anything for Sheikh Zufar al Khalia.

But not this.

The oscillation of her head grew faster as her alarm escalated. 'With respect, Your Highness, you don't want me. I'm nobody. Th-there are others far more suitable for this role. You're making a mistake.' She was a little glad that her voice held firmer than before.

Not so glad when several gasps echoed through the room and his forbidding expression tightened even further.

'I have made my decision. You are my choice. So, do you have any other objections?' he drawled.

Niesha was stunned by his question. Did that mean he would listen if she objected? What further objection could she voice other than telling the King of Khalia that he was utterly, stark raving crazy? The mere thought of doing such a thing made the blood drain from her head.

'By your silence, I assume you do not.'

'Please, you have to reconsider,' was all she could manage.

'This discussion is over,' he declared. 'But, rest assured, you will be adequately compensated for your role.'

He turned away.

Niesha knew she shouldn't trust the tiny burst of relief that spiked through her after being released from the force field of his stare. Her emotions had been on the edge of severe agitation ever since she'd walked in to find Amira and that towering barbarian of a man climbing out of the window.

She'd lost precious minutes frozen in place, unable to believe her eyes. After she'd screamed and sounded the alarm, she was sure she'd been incoherent in the first few minutes. Guilt surged anew beneath her skin.

She should've done more to stop them from leaving. Or raised the alarm quicker, as Zufar had said.

This was her punishment for not acting swiftly enough. If she had, this...*insanity* wouldn't be happening.

Because...marriage? To him?

Sweet heaven, she couldn't do it.

She took a faltering step closer to where he stood issuing clipped instructions. 'Your Highness, please, can we talk about it?' she ventured.

'We don't have time for a discussion,' he stated. His voice was soft and even, but she wasn't fooled. He was seething. 'This is an emergency requiring an interim solution. Any long-term resolutions will be thrashed out later, including whatever concerns you might have.' He went back to issuing instructions.

Heads bobbed up and down, unlike her shaking head

and her quivering body, everyone poised to move the moment he finished speaking.

Moments later, firm hands reached for her, fingers tugging insistently at her clothes. She was going to be undressed in front of him? A bolt of rebellion fired through her, and she pushed the attendants away. 'No!'

Everyone in the room froze.

'No?' Halimah whispered in horror. 'You're saying no to your King?'

A row of shocked eyes stared back at her, one in particular lasering her in place. She realised Zufar also awaited her answer. And the expression on his face was telling her everything she needed to know. There would be hell to pay if she didn't obey him. She was the one who had let Amira get away. She was the one who hadn't sounded the alarm in time. When she'd eventually done so, she'd been hysterical and inadvertently alerted the whole palace that the bride-to-be had fled.

She might not have aided his fiancée, but Amira's disappearance might have succeeded partly because of her.

Sheikh Zufar slowly retraced his steps until he towered over her. 'I too am waiting for an answer,' he breathed.

Niesha swallowed, accepting in that moment that she had very little choice. She'd helped cause this state of chaos. It was up to her to fix it.

'No,' she said. 'I...I mean yes,' she amended hurriedly when his face turned to stone. 'I will be your interim... your stand-in bride,' she whispered, her mouth bone-dry.

Niesha wasn't sure why her gaze darted to the window just then.

Sheikh Zufar followed her gaze, and, unbelievably, his face hardened even more.

'If you're thinking of going the same way as my previous bride-to-be, think again. Halimah and her companions will stay with you. They will help you to dress. You will not be left alone until you are by my side at the altar in one hour. Is that understood?'

Her world spinning ever faster on its axis, Niesha barely managed a nod of agreement.

It must've sufficed because he and his aides exited the room, Sheikh Zufar striding with the regal, animalistic grace infused in his bones since conception. There were sources that said Zufar al Khalia carried the essence of life itself with him when he moved in and out of a room.

The truth of it hit her hard as her breath was expelled in a mighty rush.

At the outer door, he paused, slashing her with golden eyes once more. 'There will be guards placed outside the doors and along every path you take today. Just to ensure that you make it from this room to the wedding ceremony without impediment.'

Niesha wanted to laugh, but she was absolutely certain that she would end up sobbing. And even she couldn't attend her wedding ceremony in tears.

Her *wedding* ceremony!

How on earth was this happening?

She had no time to dwell on it as the women sprang into action, tugging her to the centre of the room before proceeding to disrobe her. Minutes later, she found herself immersed in the rose-scented bath she had drawn for Amira only an hour or so ago.

The water was still warm, luxury gels and shampoos uncovered and ready to be used for the pre-wedding pampering the bride-to-be deserved.

The bride-to-be. *Her.*

Niesha closed her mind to the whispers swirling around her. Her emotional tank was dangerously close to full capacity for further distress. She was fairly sure Halimah and the women were speculating wildly about her. A lowly servant without a past attracted either awkward conversation or derogatory comments, no matter one's age.

Over the years, Niesha had learned to harden herself against the pitying and sometimes callous comments, but somehow the barbs always found their way to her heart. It was why she'd stopped attempting to make friends with her colleagues.

Right now, she was rawer than she'd ever felt in her life. It was almost a relief to sink into the water and let the numbness overtake her. To ignore the awkward silences and the intense loneliness drowning her and pretend this wasn't happening.

She barely felt the hands washing her body or the fingers weaving through her hair as she was cleansed from head to toe. Somewhere in the dark tunnel of despair, she realised she was still shaking, that she couldn't stop trembling even after she was bundled into a thick, luxurious robe and seated at the bridal make-up station. She stared unseeing into the middle distance as her make-up was applied and her hair dried and fussed with.

It was as they nudged her towards the wedding gown that Niesha finally woke up.

'No…' It was a feeble attempt, one a small, wounded animal seeking a last pass for mercy would make.

Of course, there was no reprieve.

'Yes,' Halimah insisted. 'For whatever reason the cosmos sees fit, you have been chosen for this role.

You will not dishonour our King by disobeying, and I will not have my head on the block because of you. Now lift up your arms so we can put this exquisite garment on you.'

Interim.

She was just an interim solution. A stand-in for today only.

Tomorrow, Zufar would go into the desert or wherever Amira had been spirited off to and bring her back.

This was temporary.

Remember this.

This time next week, she would be back in her old, familiar clothes, in her rightful place, with this terrifying incident tucked away to retell to her children and grandchildren in years to come.

They would probably not believe her, she mused numbly. She could scarcely believe it herself.

She lifted her arms and let them slide the undergarments over her body before the layers of the specially commissioned wedding gown were added. The skirt was a bit tight at the hip but the snugness wasn't uncomfortable. She held her breath as the zip was tugged up and the delicate buttons fastened.

The sensation of being sealed into her temporary prison threatened to choke her. She hurriedly blinked her prickling eyes before tears fell. Halimah wouldn't welcome her handiwork ruined, and Niesha needed to get herself back under firmer control. The quicker she was done with this, the quicker she could retreat into her shell, and life could go on again.

She placed her feet in the shoes when instructed, angled her head so the magnificent diamond and sapphire tiara could be put in place, and held her hands out for the two dozen bangles that came with the outfit. Precious gems of all shapes and sizes gleamed from her wrists, throat and ears as she was tugged forwards to stand in front of the giant gilded mirror.

Niesha only managed to hold her expression for a split second before her gaze dropped to her feet again. She didn't know the woman in the mirror. And that was a good thing. She could remove herself completely from this situation, retreat to the numb place where she was safest, away from the whispered gossip and the stunned glances. The place where the soft, kind voice lived in her head, the one she didn't recognise but had accepted over the years as her merciful companion, clinging to it the hardest when she felt her lowest.

The carers at the orphanage had offhandedly dismissed the voice she'd unwittingly confessed to as her imaginary friend. Some had ridiculed her, but Niesha had felt no shame in embracing the gentle susurration telling her she would be all right.

You'll get through this.

She was repeating those words to herself as Marwan, his aides, Halimah, and six ceremonially dressed guards escorted her down a wide private staircase towards the Rolls-Royce Phantom idling in a courtyard at the north wing of the palace. The safety of the three veils shielding her from direct view of everyone else was a welcome presence.

Still, she heard the furtive murmurs as she slowly glided forwards. Behind her, hands fluttered over her train and helped her into the car. Niesha uttered no words as Marwan slid in beside her. The part of her brain that wasn't suspended in disbelief understood his presence.

Amira's father, Feroz Ghalib, had been primed to take this role with his daughter. Even though tongues would wag at Marwan's presence beside her, it would delay the ultimate revelation of exactly what was going on.

Nevertheless, her hands trembled around the stem of the exquisite bouquet made up of diamond-studded cream roses as the car began to roll forwards.

For a wild moment, Niesha contemplated flinging open the door and fleeing as fast as her legs would carry her. She knew every nook and cranny of the royal palace, having spent all her free time exploring it over the years. She could find a hiding place within minutes.

Even as temptation seeped through her, she was dismissing it. The recent death of the Queen had devastated Khalia. The kingdom was still in mourning when its bereaved King dropped the bombshell of his abdication. Though his people had accepted Zufar wholeheartedly, aftershocks still echoed throughout the kingdom.

He'd been right when he'd said that this wedding needed to happen. Galila had said as much last night when she'd voiced her worry over Amira's curious indifference towards her wedding, leading to an exchange of words Niesha had overheard as she'd tidied up Amira's room.

There were larger implications besides a simple marriage between two people who'd known each other since childhood.

The simple truth was that Khalia could ill afford another scandal.

'Wave,' Marwan instructed tersely. 'You need to wave to the people.'

A startled glance out of the window showed they

were already on the street outside the palace. She hadn't been privy to the protocol of the ceremony but, from watching other televised royal weddings, she knew there was a brief ride to acknowledge her future subjects and show her gratitude for their goodwill, before the actual wedding ceremony began.

Slowly, she lifted her hand, her movements woefully stilted, and waved.

Screams of joy pierced the thick windows of the car, forcing home the reality that she'd become a symbol of hope to the people. She…the orphan from the poorest part of the capital, the woman with no past and no name save for the one the carers had given her.

Light-headedness clawed at the fringes of her consciousness. A garbled sound echoed from far away but she knew it had come from her throat.

'You will pull yourself together, girl,' Marwan said.

Again hysterical laughter bubbled up. How very easily everyone told her to pull herself together, to rise up to the occasion. To obey. But no one knew the terrifying depths of her emotions. No one knew how she'd secretly watched Zufar move around the palace, on TV, stared at his pictures in magazines for years. No one knew of the secret awe she held for the man who sat on the throne.

For a brief moment in her youth, she had even fancied herself in love with him! She'd grown out of that foolishness, of course, but the unfettered awareness and awe he drew from her had never dissipated.

If she'd been performing this task for any man other than the King of Khalia, she would probably have summoned something other than terror. But he wasn't any other man. Zufar al Khalia was in a stratosphere of his own, over and above the royal blood that ran through his veins and the crown that sat on his head.

All too soon the ride was over.

Trumpets sounded as the Rolls stopped in front of the Imperial Ceremonial Room where she would be taking her vows before the hour was out. The breath she drew into her lungs did nothing to offer sustenance or clarity, and, even though the senior aide highly disapproved of what was going on, Niesha was grateful for his presence as he alighted and held out his hand to her. She was certain she would've fallen into a wretched heap if he hadn't offered his support just then.

The hand she placed on his arm trembled wildly.

Flower girls she'd never met giggled and danced in front of her, throwing handfuls of scented flowers in her path as she slowly glided up the twenty-one steps to the wide doorway and down a gold-edged, royal blue carpet towards the centre of the exquisite ballroom reserved for the sole purpose of conducting official ceremonies.

Outside, several dozen more trumpets joined the heralding around the kingdom, crowds roaring where they were watching on giant screens across the city.

Inside, Niesha moved towards the man who stood tall, regal, and devastatingly handsome at the altar, her heart firmly wedged in her throat.

When Marwan winced, she realised her fingers had dug into his skin.

An apology tripped on her tongue but was immediately strangled by her nerves.

The murmurs in the congregation escalated, heads beginning to turn as speculation grew as to why Marwan walked next to the bride.

Niesha had no chance to dwell on that. Her sole focus

was on Sheikh Zufar as he swivelled on his heel to watch her progress down the aisle.

His face gave nothing away. Years under the spotlight had honed an ability to ruthlessly school his features. But the many interviews that Niesha had watched of the Crown Prince, now turned King of Khalia, had clued her into the nuances of his expressions.

Right now, he bristled with fury, still incandescent at the atrocity that had been perpetrated against him. That fury was ruthlessly caged, the greater calling of duty and responsibility taking priority. He meant to see this through, come hell or high water.

Niesha cursed her senses for choosing that moment to flare back into life. The bright colours of the Imperial Ceremonial Room, the hushed voices of the guests and the laser focus of Zufar's eyes all pierced her consciousness, grounding her mercilessly in that moment.

You will be all right.

How? she railed at the soft voice. She wanted to scream, turn and flee from the room, but there was nowhere to go. They were almost at the altar. Marwan was lowering his arm in preparation to step away.

The moment he did, Galila stepped close. Zufar's sister's face was pale, her mouth pinched as she cast a searching, bewildered glance at Niesha. Unlike the others in the room, she knew why a maidservant stood in Amira's place.

'The bouquet,' she said gently.

Niesha reluctantly handed it over, mourning the tiny support being stripped from her.

Before she could dwell on it, Zufar extended his hand. They were to take that last single step to the altar together.

Niesha stared at the long elegant fingers of her soon-to-be—temporary—husband. Automatically, she lifted her right hand and placed it in his left. She wasn't sure whether to be grateful or frightened by the pressure of the fingers that took hold of hers and nudged her forwards onto that last devastating step.

The cleric began to intone a long string of ancient words. Words that demanded obedience, fidelity, faith, companionship.

Love.

Niesha's insides scrambled over that last word. She'd known none of it in her years. The occasional kindnesses that came her way had been from strangers. In her quiet moments, she'd dreamed of such a feeling, but never in her wildest imagination had she dreamed of it being uttered in such circumstances.

A glance at Zufar showed his face was a stoic mask, the words not having any effect on him save for the façade he'd put up for the public. When it was his turn to repeat his vows he did so in deep assured tones, not hurried, not in any way nervous.

The cleric turned to Niesha. Her heart lurched frantically.

Her fingers began to tremble, then her whole body was seized by vicious little earthquakes that just wouldn't stop.

'Repeat your vows,' Zufar instructed with a grave whisper. 'Repeat them now.'

Niesha swallowed painfully, forcing her dry throat to work. She opened her mouth, and with a sense of wild surrealism said, 'I, Niesha Zalwani, take you, Zufar al Khalia, to be my husband.'

Shock waves rippled through the crowd, echoed

outside the palace as the true identity of the bride was revealed. Through it all, Zufar kept his gaze fixed, haughty, regal and straight-ahead.

'Proceed,' he commanded the cloaked cleric.

To his credit, the old man did not hesitate. He recited reams of archaic, binding words.

And a mere half an hour later, Niesha was officially wed to the King of Khalia.

CHAPTER THREE

A THREE-MINUTE STATEMENT was issued by the official press secretary on behalf of Sheikh Zufar al Khalia immediately following the ceremony. That was all it took for the strange tale of the swapped bride to turn the atmosphere from scandalised confusion into roars of elation.

By the time Niesha stood beside Zufar's side on the royal balcony above the Imperial Ceremonial Room, the whole kingdom was in a romantic frenzy. Social media went into meltdown at the idea that the King had followed his heart and married the bride of his choosing rather than the one arranged for him. The media, searching for dissenting views, had only been met with romantic sighs and tales about star-crossed lovers.

The little Niesha managed to catch only added to the surrealism of the whole thing.

A five-minute lesson in wedding protocol instead of the usual weeks of tutoring was all she'd been granted in between leaving the wedding ceremony and arriving on the balcony.

She was to stand to the right of her new husband, not the left. Her arm was never to rise above shoulder level when she waved to the crowd. And while she was allowed to show her teeth when she smiled, her demeanour should not in any way exhibit raucousness. Terse instructions whizzed through her brain, the dos and don'ts of being the new Queen streaking like lightning across her senses.

'Look straight ahead and smile,' Zufar instructed calmly. 'I believe this is the moment when you should go to your happy place and think positive thoughts.'

With everything that had unfolded in the last few hours, Niesha was terrifyingly close to succumbing to hysteria. Lately, her happy place had been curling up with a book beside the fire in her tiny bedsit on the borders of the palace grounds. Oh, how she wished she were there now. Anywhere but here, where a million eyes gawked shamelessly, and the guests of honour who were no longer bothering to keep their voices down openly speculated as to how *she* had come to be in these particular shoes.

'My happy place?' she murmured. 'I don't think that's a very good idea.'

Even though she'd kept her voice low, he heard her, and cast her a brief but hard glance.

'Why not?' he enquired. 'Isn't that what women do when they wish to escape their troubles?' There was a bitter undertone that pulled her up short but his face displayed the same neutral mask he'd worn since the moment they were announced as husband and wife, and had turned to face their honoured guests.

'I'm not sure I know what you mean,' Niesha said.

'That's not important right now. All I care about is that you do not project anything other than utter bliss to find yourself in this position. Remember, the whole world is watching.'

He probably believed he was helping. This was his

way of supporting her through an impossible situation. All Niesha could take in at that moment was the pounding of her heart and the boisterous jubilation of the crowd as they waved their flags and screamed congratulations across the royal park where they were gathered.

'Do your best. That is all I ask,' Zufar muttered. 'It would please me greatly if you did it now, however. The others are joining us.'

That was all the warning she had before the doors behind them parted and the rest of his extended family flooded onto the balcony to join them.

Galila slid into place beside her, while his brother, Malak, took his position next to Zufar. Aunts, uncles, nieces and nephews slotted into their allotted positions and acknowledged the crowd with regal waves and salutes honed into place since childhood.

While each and every one of them cast lingering looks her way.

Niesha felt thankful, for the briefest moment, that Zufar had kept her by his side. One bold relative had attempted to pry out the reason behind his last-minute change in brides. Zufar had responded with a stern rebuke for him to mind his own business.

'I will call a family gathering as soon as I have a moment to spare. But do not hold your breath. I intend to be occupied for a while with my new bride.'

His uncle had retreated with his chastised tail between his legs, while Niesha was left blushing furiously. Word had quickly spread that Sheikh Zufar was not to be questioned on the subject of his bride. Not today at least.

'I suppose congratulations are in order,' Galila murmured.

'Thank you,' Niesha replied.

'I would love to know how this interesting outcome transpired,' Galila continued. 'I mean, I left you a maid-servant. Two hours later, you're my sister-in-law. Not that I don't love a riveting story, but this—'

'Watch it, Galila,' Zufar warned beneath his breath, his hands positioned strategically in front of his face as he waved.

Galila easily maintained her graceful smile as she looked at her brother. 'What?' she asked softly. 'So sue me if I'm dying to know what happened. One minute I was attempting to locate your elusive bride-to-be and the next I seem to have acquired a new sister-in-law altogether. If I didn't know any better, I'd think I'd slipped and fallen into a reality TV show.'

'Enough,' Zufar growled. 'Don't forget there are lip-readers out there. If there's discussion to be had, we will get to it later. For now, remember where you are.'

Beside him, his brother Malak snorted under his breath. 'If you wanted us to behave, brother, you shouldn't have offered us this salacious piece of adventure on your wedding day. If you're trying to get into the history books, then bravo. No one will forget this day in a hurry.'

The only hint that Zufar wasn't in complete control of his emotions was the small tic that throbbed at his temple. He continued to wave and acknowledge the crowd, and even at one point slid his hand around the Niesha's waist as the royal military jets flew overhead.

Niesha was thankful for the deafening roar of the jet engines, as it swallowed the gasp that travelled through her body when his hand settled on the curve of her waist. Besides the moment when he'd helped her off the floor, and the moment he'd slid the wedding ring onto her finger, Zufar hadn't touched her.

She'd been very thankful for that, she told herself, despite the humiliating stone lodged in her stomach when he'd lifted her veils and promptly stepped away without executing the customary newly-wed altar kiss.

But now, with his touch searing through the folds of the wedding gown right into her skin, Niesha couldn't suppress the tingles that swarmed her body. The smile she'd pinned to her face froze as her every sense homed in on the sensation evoked by his touch. It was as if his hand were charged with a unique voltage that zinged through her bloodstream, firing up little explosions of fireworks. A handful of seconds passed, then more, and then all sense of time and space disappeared as Zufar looked down into her eyes.

Tawny-gold eyes seared right into her soul, as if he intended to possess her every thought. Somewhere in the distance the royal jets performed acrobatic loops, and then started their return journey. She knew it was only a matter of moments before millions of confetti pieces would be tossed from the sky and showered upon them.

It was the moment the crowd had been waiting for.

The moment when the King kissed his new Queen.

Never in her wildest dreams had she believed it would be her. Above that, never in her wildest dreams had she believed that a man like Zufar would be staring down at her with that intense look in his eyes.

It was all an act, she repeated to herself. But her hammering heart and the frenzied little cyclones whirling through her veins dared to suggest otherwise. His hand steered her to face him, an insistent move that told her that there was no getting away from this. Zufar, the man she'd harboured silly dreams about in her teenage years, was about to kiss her.

Far above her head, a gigantic burst of blues and golds rained from the sky. Niesha paid little attention. Every single cell in her body was focused on the head slowly lowering towards hers, the hand grasping her waist, and the firm, insistent tug as he pulled her close.

'Relax,' he breathed, his voice holding warning as well as rough reassurance.

But Niesha wasn't reassured. How many women dreamed that their very first kiss would be witnessed by millions, if not billions of people across the world? What if she got it wrong? What if she made a complete fool of herself, more than she had before this whole debacle started? And what if—

'Niesha,' Zufar murmured again, his warning deeper this time.

'I'm trying,' she whispered back fiercely.

'Try harder. You look as if you are heading for the gallows instead of your first kiss with your new husband. Is kissing me such a daunting prospect?' he drawled.

'Maybe it is. Have you considered that it may be the last thing I want?'

His eyes widened a touch with surprise at the spark of defiance in her voice.

Tawny-gold eyes gleamed an instant before the first shower of confetti drifted past her. Another landed on her cheek.

About to brush it away, she froze when he murmured, 'Stop.'

He captured her free hand, the one not holding the bouquet, and laid it gently on his chest. And then, with a suave move, he brushed the tiny gold piece of tinsel from her cheek. Expecting his hand to return to her waist, Niesha gave a little gasp as his fingers stroked her jaw and then drifted to her neck.

This wasn't how it was supposed to go. She'd seen more than a few royal first kisses, had dreamed many years ago of how it would feel to be the recipient of one, just like any other girl her age.

Those embraces had been chaste, the exchanged gazes nowhere near this intense.

Zufar was breaking protocol.

But, of course, she couldn't question his actions. Not without risking her lips being read. So she stood before him, attempting not to tremble out of her skin as sure fingers drew down her neck to rest lightly on her collarbone. His thumb gently tilted her chin upward, causing her shiver to intensify.

'How you tremble so, little one,' Zufar murmured.

She opened her mouth—to say what, she would never know. Because in that moment Zufar closed the gap between them and sealed his lips on hers.

The roar and the call of trumpets were for this staged show, Niesha knew. But every sound intensified the thrill and sizzle in her blood the moment Zufar kissed her. She wasn't sure why she closed her eyes, but it felt like the right thing to do. Perhaps because she was more than a little drugged from the effect of his mouth on hers.

It was like nothing she'd ever experienced in her life. Heat and magic and earth-shaking desire surged through her body, flowing from his lips right through to her very toes. He swallowed her tiny squeak of shocked delight as he deepened the kiss. His hand didn't move from her throat but the one at her waist dug deeper, searing his fingers onto her skin. That tiny moan escaped again. The crowd roared louder. All through it Zufar continued to kiss her, his tongue swiping across her bottom lip, weakening her knees so she sagged against him.

He caught her easily, held onto her as he continued to gently ravage her mouth.

'Enough, you two,' Galila said with a chuckle. 'There are children watching. Let's not turn this into an X-rated show.'

With a muted grunt, Zufar lifted his head. His face reflected a hint of surprise, then irritated bewilderment. Both were quickly masked a moment later.

If it had been anyone else, she would've believed he was experiencing the same sensations cascading through her body, but his eyes studied her with piercing speculation that added apprehension to her already jangled emotions.

What was he thinking?

As if he caught the silent question, his hand dropped from her throat, and he faced the crowd. A smile lifted the corners of his mouth, as if he was acknowledging that he'd just shared a special moment with every citizen in his kingdom, and millions more around the world. A second later, he looked down at her, his eyes telling her that she needed to also acknowledge the crowd.

Blushing fiercely, Niesha faced the crowd again. In unison, they waved, smiled, waved some more. All the while, her senses spun.

Her first kiss.

Was this how everyone felt? She was drowning in sensation, as if the whole world had tilted and taken a different course that would never be the same again. Because how could anything else compare to this?

She wasn't a romantic. Childish, fairy-tale feelings had been beaten out of her by years of hard work and the reality that only a lucky few found their happily-ever-after, most of them in the books she treasured. She was old enough to accept that those foolish daydreams needed to be set aside the moment she closed the book.

So what she was experiencing now was nothing short of a daydream she needed to put behind her as soon as possible.

This was temporary. *She was a stand-in.*

Come tomorrow she'd be back in her beige uniform, fluffing pillows and refilling shampoo bottles in bathrooms in the east wing.

The thought froze the smile on her face, even as she continued to wave to the crowd.

After an excruciating half-hour, with one final wave, Zufar steered her away from the balcony. They reentered the small anteroom serving as a holding place before, but that was now a path that led to the banqueting hall where the formal wedding reception was being held.

'You did well,' Zufar stated as he tucked her hand into the crook of his elbow.

Despite the tersely murmured statement, a bubble of warmth speared through the sizzling shock that hadn't entirely left her.

'Thank you,' she murmured, pleased that she hadn't completely let him down.

'Of course, you could do with smiling a little bit more,' he added.

The bubble burst. 'I can't smile on command,' she replied.

'You are the Queen now. You have to learn how.'

'But I am not, though, am I?'

'That ring on your finger, my dear, is all the evidence you need.'

'You know what I mean, Your Highness.'

'Do I?' Zufar murmured even as he nodded to a guest bowing as they passed.

'Of course you do,' Niesha muttered fiercely. Why was he pretending he didn't know what she was talking about? 'I'm not your Queen. This was temporary. You said so yourself.'

His body tensed, then a muscle rippled in his jaw. 'We'll talk about this later,' he said.

A spurt of apprehension turned into full-blown alarm. 'What is there to talk about, Your Highness?'

'You calling me Your Highness, for starters. I'm your husband now. You are allowed to address me as Zufar.'

Her footsteps faltered. For as long as she could remember, he'd always been Sheikh Zufar, or Crown Prince Zufar. Not even in her dreams had she addressed him by his given name alone. It felt…huge. As if she were taking a leap into thin air. Niesha started to shake her head.

Somehow, she had to bring this back to reality, back under her control.

'You also need to stop shaking your head at every little disagreement. As my new bride, you're supposed to be glowing and blushing with happiness, not wearing an expression as if you've been led into the devil's own playpen.'

'You know why I am acting this way. I don't know

why you're pretending you don't know what I'm talking about. You said this was temporary.'

'Did I?'

Her mouth parted in a stunned O.

'Remember where you are,' he warned. 'Do you really think this is the right time for this discussion?'

She didn't. And she couldn't very well demand an explanation from the King. Not with guests in earshot, and not when they were entering the banqueting hall where attendants lined the walls in their dozens, ready to serve the first course the moment they sat down.

So she walked beside him as Zufar led her to the head of the table.

His white-gloved hand gripped hers tightly where it rested on his arm, as if he was fully intent on preventing her from fleeing.

As if she would. As if she *could*. She wouldn't get very far, even on her own two feet. As he'd warned, there were guards posted everywhere in the palace. Did his warning still apply even now that they'd exchanged their vows? Most likely. But she couldn't think about that. All she wanted at this moment was for everything to be done so she could disappear into her little corner of the world and put this behind her. But he was looking at her in that way again as the guests crowded in.

The way he'd looked at her on the balcony in the moments before he'd kissed her. It was all still an act, Niesha knew. But that tiny fluttering reignited under her skin and grew into huge, wild butterflies demanding freedom.

When the room was half filled, he pulled out her chair and waited until she sat down. He remained standing, his gaze on the crowd who stood as protocol demanded, beside their seats.

Zufar's gaze effortlessly commanded their attention. 'Many of you are wondering about the turn of events today. You will have to keep wondering.' A smattering of laughter echoed through the crowd but eyes slid to where she sat, probing her every expression in the hope of accessing juicy gossip. It took every ounce of composure she didn't know she possessed to maintain a serene expression as Zufar continued, 'All you need to know is that I've made my choice, and I am extremely happy with it.'

Her pulse jumped as he redirected his gaze to her again, his eyes gleaming for a moment before he straightened. 'Now you will do me the honour of acknowledging and accepting Niesha al Khalia as my bride and your Queen.'

Thunderous applause echoed down the banqueting table. Then they took their seats and the formal reception began.

Niesha only managed to pick at a few mouthfuls of the twelve-course dinner. Aside from a few sidelong glances, Zufar didn't question her lack of appetite. She supposed it could all be slotted under the general heading of wedding nerves, even after the fact.

And almost as if he'd instituted an invisible no-fly zone around her, no one approached her even to offer congratulations.

When Galila breached the barrier, Zufar shot her a warning look.

She rolled her eyes but didn't make any more comments except to lean down and brush a kiss across Niesha's cheek. 'You and I will need to have a spa day very soon,' she whispered in Niesha's ear before straightening and walking away.

'What did she say?' Zufar asked.

'She wants a spa day with me, I think,' Niesha responded a little dazedly.

'Hmm, I believe that is code for something else entirely.'

Surprise rounded her eyes. 'What?'

'Curiosity is my sister's middle name. I will caution you to be careful around her. She has a way of prying out information that would make my own intelligence department proud.'

She reached for the crystal water glass, aware that her fingers hadn't stopped shaking. 'Well, you don't need to worry about that, do you? By the time we get around to the possibility of such a day, I'll no longer be your wife.'

For some reason her response made his features tighten. Did he not wish to hear the truth? She opened her mouth to voice the thought but he beat her to it.

'This is our wedding day. Let us endeavour to enjoy at least some of it and not give everything a sour note, shall we?'

She frowned, then quickly smoothed out her features, aware that she was still the cynosure of all eyes. 'It's not our wedding day. Not really. Is it?' she pressed, intent on making him acknowledge the transient nature of what had happened today.

It was that or... The alternative was unthinkable. No, not exactly unthinkable, but impossible for someone like her. A nobody who'd left such foolish dreams beneath the dreary pillows in her lonely orphanage bed.

'Think of it as an elaborate party then, if you must,'

he bit out quietly. 'Whatever it is, I wish to enjoy at least some of it for the sake of appearances. Is that okay with you?'

Was he really asking her that when he'd all but dragged her to the altar? But the anger she wanted to summon didn't materialise. Not when she knew the true meaning behind his actions.

He'd done it for his people. So had she. She owed it to the royal family and to every citizen in Khalia not to sustain that anger. She didn't need to be in his shoes to understand it took guts to take such chaos as had been thrown at him only a few hours ago, a situation that would've left other men quaking in their boots, and turn it into a triumph.

Proving once again why he was such an effective, awe-inspiring monarch.

One who had demanded a sacrifice she couldn't in good conscience fault him for. Right in this moment, Niesha couldn't find it in her heart to begrudge the people of Khalia, who had endured the death of their Queen, and seen the kingdom plunged into uncertainty after the abdication of the King.

'Of course, if that's what you wish,' she murmured softly.

His eyes gleamed in that suspicious way again, as if he were divining her thoughts way better than she could. It made her *extremely* nervous. Niesha attempted to look away, but found herself hypnotised by the gold flecks in his tawny eyes.

'That is what I wish,' he reiterated in deep, low tones. 'Now you will smile, and nod, and pretend that this is the happiest day of your life.'

For some insane reason, that command wasn't difficult to obey.

When the corners of his mouth lifted, Niesha found herself following suit. His gaze dropped to her lips, and stayed there for an infinitesimal second, before he lifted his gaze back to hers.

'Much better,' he drawled. 'I will push my luck and request that you eat more than the few mouthfuls you have consumed so far. If the food does not suit, you only need to say and I will instruct a new dish to be brought to you.'

Her eyes widened. What would her peers—the servants—think if she made such a request? She cringed. 'No, that will not be necessary.'

'I do not do it out of necessity. I do it because you are my Queen and what you wish goes.'

What she *wished* right now was for him to stop referring to her as the Queen or *his* Queen. It would be better all round that way. *Safer*, even. The last thing she wanted was to start believing, even for a second that this temporary role was in any way real. She needed to maintain the distance to ensure she left this nightmare with her faculties intact. 'This is fine, I'm sure,' she insisted firmly.

Zufar nodded, and turned to speak to his brother, who sat to his left. The sudden bereft sensation that assailed her took Niesha by complete surprise. It took a few precious seconds to master her composure, after which she lifted her gaze to the guest seated closest by. But that chair was empty, vacated by Galila a few moments ago.

She was about to turn away, but her attention was snagged by Zufar's uncle, the same one who'd attempted to pry information from Zufar earlier. Niesha attempted a smile. He returned it with a speculative gaze, his eyes darting from Zufar and back again.

'You must come to dinner when you return from your honeymoon.'

Honeymoon?

She tried to master the shock that bolted through her.

Of course the King and Queen were expected to go on their honeymoon. She had no clue where Zufar had intended to take Amira. Was she supposed to know of the destination for her own honeymoon?

'I...I...' she stuttered. A moment later, a warm hand covered hers, the gentle but insistent pressure on her fingers applying subtle warning.

'We'll be happy to accept your invitation, Uncle, on our return. Providing of course that our schedules allow,' Zufar slid in smoothly, proving that even though he'd been in conversation with his brother, he had been fully tuned into what was happening with her.

Was he that terrified she would bungle the ruse? A spark of irritation lit up beneath her skin. When she attempted to withdraw her hand from under his, he held on firmly, turning his imperious head to look at her with what everyone else would have assumed was an adoring look from a groom to his new bride. But she saw the warning clear in his eyes. *Behave.*

She lowered her head under the guise of forking another bite of her superb sea bass. But she never lifted it to her lips, because she feared she would choke if she attempted to swallow.

'Where's the honeymoon destination?' the woman seated next to Zufar's uncle asked.

'We will spend a few days in the Emerald Palace,

and then I will take my bride on a multi-national tour, ending in the most romantic capital of the world, of course,' Zufar said.

'Oh, you mean Paris, don't you? I love Paris,' his aunt exclaimed, her eyes lighting up. 'I haven't been in months.'

'And there's a reason for that,' his uncle said dryly. 'My bank account screams in agony whenever you're in the French capital.'

Laughter greeted the response. Amid it all, Niesha noticed Zufar watching her with that same pseudo-adoring, warning look. When his uncle turned away to address another guest, she tried to withdraw her hand once again.

Even though her irritation had faded, a new sensation had taken root at his touch. He no longer wore his gloves, making the sensation even more searing. The burst of relief poured through her when he didn't restrain her. She dropped her hand into her lap, her fingers curling into her palm as her blood sang wildly.

Realising that he was still staring at her, she pinned that smile on her face again, and returned his look. 'You don't need to keep watching me like a hawk, you know. I'm not about to announce to the whole world what is happening here.'

'I'm glad to hear it, but since we did not discuss a honeymoon, I thought it best to step in. Surely you don't have an objection to that?' he murmured testily.

'But what will they say when they find out that it's not true?' she said tightly.

The taut little smile he gave her reproached her for being foolish. 'That will not happen, little one, because it's true. We are going on honeymoon.'

* * *

Zafar had never met anyone who blushed with such frequency as his new bride. Or trembled as much. He was stunned she hadn't collapsed into a heap of nerves thus far. His earlier summation that she was as skittish as one of his mares couldn't be more accurate. Even now, as they took their first dance, he sensed she was moments from tugging out of his hold and fleeing across the ballroom.

But just like before, right when he thought she would succumb to her nerves, she straightened her slender spine, raised that delicate little chin, and speared him with a look of such defiance it almost made him smile.

Almost.

Because this was no laughing matter. He had taken a complete stranger as his Queen. Granted, Amira had been little more than an acquaintance despite the arrangement to marry, but this was…unprecedented.

Just like that kiss on the balcony…

He clenched his gut as the memory drew another strange zing through his bloodstream. It had just been a kiss, nothing more. So why was the unique sensation lingering, luring him into wishing to experience it again? He wouldn't, of course.

This whole near disaster had him on edge. The adrenaline high of salvaging a situation that could've exploded in his face was what had blown that kiss out of proportion.

But it was time to wrestle *everything* back under control.

Despite the press release holding at bay the dozens of questions he was sure were coming his way, his people would need definitive answers by morning.

He'd barely been able to stop Amira's father from detonating the whole event even before it'd started. The man was rightly in search of answers for his daughter's whereabouts and bewildered at the news that Amira had jilted the man she was supposed to marry. Only by asserting his full authority had Zufar stopped his father's best friend from causing a scene. Feroz had finally realised Zufar was the wronged party and agreed to return home to await further news.

Zufar resisted the urge to grit his teeth at the thought of his half-brother's actions.

He had set his best investigators on the case to satisfy himself that Amira hadn't been taken against her will, but instinctively he knew she hadn't been abducted. In fact, in hindsight, Amira's lacklustre interaction with him lately was revelatory.

That sliver of relief slid through him again, this time arriving with a cold acceptance that perhaps he'd dodged a bullet that could've seen history repeating itself. Because a wife that could've so easily been seduced by another man, as his mother had been, was one he didn't want. Maybe his half-brother had done him a favour. Had even unwittingly ensured Zufar wasn't distracted from his duty and responsibility the way his father's preoccupation with his mother's infidelity had made him?

His teeth met in jaw-clenching grit. He wasn't so forgiving as to brush away the fact that Adir had done this *today* to extract maximum humiliation—

'Perhaps you should take your own advice, Your Highness,' his new bride stated softly.

He redirected his gaze to hers. 'Excuse me?'

'You want me to smile and not give the game away but you should see your face right now,' she said.

'And what does my face say?'

'That you are terribly displeased by something. Of course, I'm sure I don't need to guess what it is. You think you will find her soon?' she asked.

He pushed his irritation away. 'I don't wish to talk about Amira.' Further thought of his half-brother was not welcome. Moreover, Zufar found he was much more interested in the woman he held in his arms.

For the purposes of keeping in character, of course.

Because Niesha was right. He was at risk of giving the game away. He schooled his features as he continued to look down at her. As he did so, he noticed the changes in her.

The hair he'd believed to be mousy was in fact a lustrous thick chestnut, highlighted with dark gold strands he was sure didn't come out of a tube. Her eyelashes were unbelievably long, fanning almost hypnotically against her cheeks when she lowered them. Lips painted a deep peach drew his eyes consistently to the soft, plump curve of her mouth. Her eyes were wide and alluring pools edged in kohl that emphasised the amethyst depths.

In her heels, she came up to his chin, bringing him that much closer to the lips he had tasted all too briefly on the balcony outside. Lips that his own thirsted to taste.

The zing threatened to spark into something else, something *more* as his recollection deepened.

She wasn't experienced, that much he could tell by kissing her, but he had sensed an innocent eagerness in her that lit a fire in his belly. The temptation to kiss her, experience that thrill again, fanned his hunger. He curbed it ruthlessly.

He wasn't weak like his father, controlled by his obsessional urges to the ruin of all else around him. Zufar enjoyed sex, and the carefully selected women he'd indulged himself with over the years had more than satisfied his needs. But not a single time had he let his emotions overtake him.

He didn't intend to start now.

Duty had dictated he take a wife and produce heirs. That would be his end goal. And with Amira out of the picture…

He stared at his new Queen. His *temporary* Queen.

His people's reaction to her had been…extraordinary. Surprisingly so. They'd readily accepted her. So why upset the cart?

Why indeed…?

Zufar cautioned himself against revealing to Niesha that, far from thinking that this was only a temporary marriage, she was now bound to him for life. That conversation would need careful strategising.

In the same instance that he accepted his decision, it occurred to him that the idea of binding himself to a near stranger neither disturbed nor displeased him. He'd never intended to marry for anything other than ensuring lasting stability for his people after the turbulence of his father's reign.

He wasn't so weak as to give into ephemeral notions of marrying for love. That emotion was a fairy tale he'd never wasted his time seeking, and especially not once the reality of his position in life had been made clear.

His father had fallen victim to lust and obsession to the detriment of his family and his kingdom. Zufar was well aware of the whispers that had followed his father, the veiled scorn shown towards the weakness that dogged the previous King. He had no intention of falling prey to that absurd sickness.

'I'm in no hurry to locate my former fiancée.'

Her breath caught. 'And why not?'

'Because if she went of her own free will, then she's no longer of any consequence.'

She gasped. 'How can you say that? She was promised to you. You still need a bride! Your people need a queen.'

Zufar continued to look down at her as they glided across the dance floor. Absent-mindedly, he noted the grace with which she swayed in his arms, the way she held herself with careful poise. She wasn't as unpolished as he'd imagined, he mused again. In fact, with a little bit of help, she could become the diamond he sought. The diamond his people deserved.

The more he thought about it, the more the idea settled deeper inside him.

'Your Highness?' Her prompt was tremulous, as if she knew of the monumental decision he'd taken.

Her eyes were growing wide again, her lower lip set to tremble in that alluring quiver that made him want to devour her again.

'I don't need to find her, little one, because I've already found my bride. I've found my Queen. This wedding, and this marriage, will be my first and my last. There hasn't been a divorce in my family in recorded history. In fact, I'm not sure the constitution has allowances for it. So, you see, you and I are bound together for life, Niesha. Accept it.'

CHAPTER FOUR

IF NIESHA HAD been informed only half an hour ago that there was a way for her whole world to be shoved even more off kilter, she wouldn't have believed it. But she was fully installed on that wild, turbulent roller coaster now.

She stared up at Zufar, knowing that this time there was no mistaking what he'd said. Nor was there any doubt that this was an accidental revelation. They were in the middle of the dance floor, surrounded by over three hundred guests. She had nowhere to go, was unable to protest without causing the most horrendous scene.

Zufar al Khalia's diplomatic prowess and mental agility was renowned. He'd won almost every polo match since he was seventeen. The moment he'd entered public office, he'd gained a reputation as a master strategist.

That he'd brought those abilities to bear on this situation was irrefutable. Panic and anger surged in her belly, lending her vocal cords the strength to dig herself out of this hole she was disappearing into.

He shook his head. 'Not here,' he instructed tersely.

'You lied to me,' she whispered, the depth of his trap making her tone husky with shock.

His eyes grew chilly but the smile didn't fade from

his face. 'I said, not here,' he emphasised with clear displeasure.

But Niesha was a little too out of her head to heed the warning. 'You planned this all along.'

'If you mean did I plan to speak to you afterwards so we can discuss this like rational human beings, then yes, that was my intention.'

Chilled through by his almost careless dismissal, she took a step back from him, but the arm banding her waist pulled her closer, the fingers curled around hers holding her prisoner. 'You will not cause a scene.'

Her King demanded obedience. But in that moment, Niesha couldn't find the capacity to fall in line like everyone else at his command.

'You keep telling me how to behave, to smile, to breathe. I'm not an object, Your Highness. I'm a human being. I chose to obey you because I thought I was doing the right thing. But you misled me. I will not stand for that.'

His nostrils flared, his whole being tightening against her as his gaze pinned her.

'What is it you're intending to do?' he questioned with a deadly smile.

'I won't cause a scene, if that's what you are worried about.'

A single tic rippled through his jaw before he regained himself. 'That's good to hear. However, I hear a *but* in there.'

'I will remain meekly by your side until this ceremony is over. And then you and I will talk.'

One corner of his mouth lifted in a hint of a smile that promised to be lethal given its full scope. 'My meek little bride seems to have a spine after all,' he mocked.

The bubble of anger in Niesha's belly grew. 'I get that way when I'm misled.'

'Be careful. Don't forget whom you're addressing,' he warned.

A chill went through her body. 'Is that a threat, Your Highness?'

'I am reminding you that we have an audience, and our every move is being watched so if you are going to be disagreeable, I suggest you wait until we are behind closed doors.'

'Disagreeable? You think I'm being—'

Before she could further vent her anger, he leaned close and brushed his lips over hers.

Like on the balcony, this was meant to shut her up. Niesha knew that. And yet it worked like magic. The high-wattage shiver that went down her spine was so strong she thought she would be lifted right off her feet.

And that was with just a whisper of his lips over hers. She cursed her body's reaction. Continued cursing it as the song ended and she was led off the ballroom floor with suave attentiveness.

As if he knew and meant to capitalise on her reaction to his touch, Zufar didn't release her. Long fingers meshed with hers as they moved from group to group holding brief court with their guests.

For two hours she was subjected to his electrifying touch and blasts from tawny eyes that held her fraying nerves on a tight leash.

The evening culminated with spectacular fireworks on the great lawn of the palace. Across the capital city, individual households joined in, with bursts of fireworks lighting the sky across the city.

Niesha barely acknowledged them. All she wanted

to do was to retreat at the earliest opportunity and guarantee her fate wasn't as final as she suspected.

Relief drenched her as her attendants materialised beside her at the stroke of nine p.m. to whisk her off. Moments later, she realised Zufar was not following as she'd expected.

She stopped. They needed to discuss what he'd said now. She couldn't bear to wait another second. 'Wait. I need to—'

He intercepted her as she headed back to where he stood with one of his ministers. 'Go on without me. We will be reunited soon enough, little one,' he said smoothly as he took her hand and brushed his lips over her knuckles.

Dear heaven, he was smooth.

And calculating.

She was struggling to find her breath when the women firmly led her away.

Niesha was so caught up in the conversation she intended to have with him that she didn't notice where they were headed until she realised that they weren't returning to the Queen's private quarters. 'What... Where are you taking me?' she blurted, although she had a fair idea.

Halimah, walking a few steps in front of her, looked over her shoulder and smiled. This time her smile was more tactful, her whole demeanour remarkably altered from this morning.

Of course, Niesha mused, she was now the Queen, and where there'd been whispered speculation and awkwardness before, there were now smiles and an abundance of courtesy and respect.

Even as a tiny spurt of resentment erupted inside her

for their about-face, she wanted to blurt out that there was no need for their change of attitude. She was still one of them. She certainly wasn't going to be Queen for very long, not if she had any say in it.

The thought that her wish might not come true sent a fresh bolt of alarm through her. Zufar hadn't misspoken. Niesha didn't know the ins and outs of constitutional law, but she knew the history of the royal family enough to know that there'd been no divorce for generations.

To date, Zufar's own father had been the only one to abdicate the throne and that had sent shock waves through the kingdom.

'Your Highness?'

Niesha whirled around, expecting Zufar to be behind her. When he wasn't, she turned back around, frowning at Halimah.

'Your Highness, which gown do you prefer?' the attendant urged.

She realised that she was the one being addressed, and her heart lurched. 'Please, don't call me that.'

Halimah and the young attendants exchanged apprehensive looks. 'Begging your pardon, but that is your official title. To address you as anything else would be disrespectful, Your Highness.'

'I see,' Niesha replied. Her resentment of moments before dissipated, replaced with the stark notion that, whether she liked it or not, they truly saw her differently now. She might not feel it inside but to them she was now a rarefied species, no longer one of them. Niesha didn't know whether to be sad or to give into more hysteria. She settled for a solemn nod. 'Okay.' She knew how rigorously the rules of the palace were followed. The last thing she wanted to do was cause trouble for the staff. She would be one of them again soon enough.

'I've prepared some tea for Your Highness. Jasmine tea, to calm the nerves before the wedding night,' Halimah offered with a benign smile.

Niesha stopped herself from blurting that it was a waste of time. She didn't intend to sleep in Zufar's private quarters tonight or on any other night.

'Can you help me with my gown, please?'

'Of course, Your Highness,' Halimah sang out.

Gentle hands began undoing her clothing. She wasn't sure why she paid closer attention this time. Perhaps it was the knowledge that she would never be close to such perfect creations again that made her look down at her gown properly for the first time, noticing the precious stones sewn into the skirts swirling around her legs as it was removed, the delicate sleeves and masterful design.

An exquisite diamond and sapphire necklace gleamed against her skin, the gems in her ears and on her wrist adding to the magical quality of the wedding gown that didn't belong to her and never would.

But for one small infinitesimal moment, she allowed herself to believe that this was real.

When she finally met her gaze in the mirror, she dared to dream that when this moment was far behind her, she would one day experience a wedding day of her own.

Smaller and less spectacular, of course, but enchanted all the same.

First, though, she had to get through to Zufar. Had to extricate herself from this web of impossible circumstances closing in on her. She raised her arms as the gown was lifted over her head and spirited away.

Then Halimah was in front of her, gesturing to an array of gorgeous evening gowns hanging from a rail.

Niesha stared at the dresses in surprise. 'Are these new?' They hadn't been there this morning and she hadn't spotted them with the bridal trousseau.

Halimah nodded. 'His Highness ordered these for you himself.'

'Excuse me?' she blurted.

A smile curved Halimah's lips. 'The suddenness of the…new arrangements left you no choice but to wear the only wedding gown available. But I believe your new husband did not wish to see you in another woman's clothes on the night of your wedding. He had the royal couturier provide these for you especially.' There was wistfulness in Halimah's voice that suggested that underneath the sometimes brusque exterior lurked a romantic.

Nevertheless, Niesha was stunned Zufar had arranged all this. Should she really be surprised? If the bombshell he'd dropped on the dance floor was true, then within minutes of entering this room this afternoon he'd made a life-altering decision for her without so much as blinking in her direction.

The formidable calculation behind that staggered her.

'Which one is it to be, Your Highness?' Halimah prompted.

Half dazed, Niesha pointed to the emerald sequinned gown, made of material she was almost too afraid to touch. 'That one,' she murmured.

'A wonderful choice, Your Highness,' Halimah agreed.

That bubble of hysteria threatened again. She swallowed it down, willing herself to remain quiet as the women bustled around her again.

Her hair was rearranged, her make-up touched up, and heels presented to her.

'We thought you would prefer your tea on the terrace, Your Highness. The fireworks are still going on, and you can get the best view from there.'

Niesha trailed after them out onto a stone terrace where an elaborate tea service had been laid out. She'd barely eaten anything at the wedding banquet but Niesha knew she wouldn't be able to eat now either. She contemplated the exquisite offering, wondering whether she shouldn't try anyway to calm her nerves.

But she didn't want her nerves calmed. She'd been too dazed and confused earlier, had meekly stumbled her way through what should've been a firm refusal to succumb to his wishes. She'd gone along with the idea that she would be a stand-in, temporary bride. She intended to make her voice heard this time.

She would scream if she needed to. With a brisk nod to herself, Niesha sat down and held her hands in her lap.

'May I pour you a cup, Your Highness?'

She stopped herself from gritting her teeth at the title. It didn't belong to her and she would never get used to it.

'No, thank you,' she said. 'You may go now. I'll pour it myself when I am ready.'

'But… Your Highness, that is not protocol.'

Niesha swallowed her irritation. 'I'm quite capable of pouring my own tea, Halimah.'

The older woman gave a curt bow, and stepped back. 'As you wish, Your Highness. Will there be anything else?'

Niesha shook her head. But as the women started to retreat, she turned. 'Do you know when Zu—His Highness will be here?' She heard the nervousness in her own voice but Halimah's gaze only softened.

'You can expect him within the hour, Your Highness.'

Another series of curtsies later, Niesha was alone.

An hour.

She snorted under her breath. The likelihood that she would've gone completely mad by then was very real. The moment she heard the door shut, she jumped to her feet.

There had to be a way out of this, there simply had to be. She paced until her feet began to pinch, and then she kicked the shoes off. Hearing them thud against the wall brought a tiny bit of satisfaction, immediately followed by guilt at the treatment of what had to be thousands of dollars' worth of accessories.

That thought ramped up her agitation. As she turned from her pacing, another burst of fireworks lit through the sky. Niesha lifted her head to watch it, the enormity of why this celebration was happening settling on her. She raised a hand to her throbbing head and caught a spark of her wedding ring. It was unlike any ring she'd ever seen.

From the history of the al Khalia kingdom she'd devoured back in her teens she knew exactly where the ring on her finger had originated. It had belonged to Zufar's grandmother. She'd been married to his grandfather for over seventy years and had worn the ring every day of her married life. The heirloom's historical significance threatened to overwhelm her. Perhaps it was fortunate then that the hard rap on the outer door dragged her from her thoughts.

The bundle of nerves that jumped into her throat suggested perhaps not. On shaky feet, she rushed to where she'd thrown off her shoes and slipped back into the heels. Sucking in a deep breath, she walked through the living room to the doors. With one last slide of her clammy palms over her dress, Niesha opened the doors.

Zufar too had changed. Gone was the magnificent military uniform he'd worn for the ceremony. In its place was an equally captivating tunic that drew her eyes to his broad shoulders and the tapered physique that been honed from his love of polo. Dark curly hair gleamed under the chandelier lights. He'd taken a shower at some point since she'd last seen him.

Despite the emotions raging inside her, Niesha couldn't take her eyes off him. The subtle clearing of his throat embarrassingly long seconds later alerted her to her gawping.

When she met his gaze, his eyes were a touch cool, but as his gaze roved from her head down to her feet a different look replaced it. A look that sent hot tingles surging through her belly to curl low and insistent in her pelvis.

'Are you going to invite me in or do you wish to tackle me where I stand?'

Niesha cursed the blush spreading in her cheeks, and stepped back hastily. He stepped inside and shut the door behind him.

'The gown suits you,' he said with more than a hint of satisfaction.

The thought that he'd chosen it especially for her shouldn't have sent that traitorous bolt of pleasure through her bloodstream, and Niesha immediately wished it away. She didn't want to speak about clothes. Or wonder whether the unbelievably soft and silky gown that clung to her breasts, waist and hips pleased him in any way. She only wanted to talk about her freedom.

'Tell me what you said isn't true,' she blurted heatedly.

He didn't respond but his nostrils flared slightly as he looked around the room. 'Perhaps we should sit down.'

Niesha shook her head. 'No. You said this was an *interim* solution. I want to know why you deceived me,' she demanded, her voice more plaintive than she wished.

'Calm yourself.' His voice was a firm command.

'I'll be calm when you tell me that this marriage will be annulled as soon as possible,' she returned.

He didn't react to the unbecoming screech in her voice or the undeniable accusation she lobbed at him. He merely continued to stride away from her towards the living room, leaving her no choice but to follow.

She watched him lower his impressive frame into the heavy silk armchair she was sure cost more than two years' salary, and cross one leg over the other.

'I've had you investigated,' he stated baldly. 'You do not have any family, correct?'

A bolt of pain shot through her heart, along with the shock of discovering he was changing tactic yet again.

With balled fists, she stared at him. 'You had me investigated?' she parroted.

He nodded calmly, as if her incredulity was of no consequence to him. Perhaps it wasn't. But the thought that while they'd been exchanging vows he'd been digging into her background made nausea rise in her belly.

Knowing what he'd found, knowing that he had evidence that she was a nobody, literally and figuratively, sent another wave of anguish through her.

Nonetheless, she raised her chin. 'Then you'll have your confirmation that I'm unsuitable for this…this…'

'Being my Queen?' he finished softly. So softly she barely heard the words.

Why was he so calm? Why was he not doing everything in his power to be rid of her at the first opportunity?

'Yes,' she hissed, taking a step closer to him even though her instincts warned that it would be wiser to keep a sensible distance between them.

'On the contrary, I believe it is to my advantage.'

'Your advantage?' she echoed blankly.

'Precisely. I have no relatives to appease, no scandals to come out of the woodwork. There is only you to deal with,' he stated with faint satisfaction.

Her heart lurched. 'What exactly do you mean by that?'

His gaze raked over her again, lingering longer this time. As if he had all the time in the world. 'You've had a challenging day, little one. Sit down before you fall down.'

Niesha barely managed to stop herself from stomping her feet. 'I'm not as weak as you think I am. I'm perfectly capable of carrying on a conversation without needing to wilt into the nearest chair.'

'But perhaps it will be more civil that way?' he parried in a mocking tone before flicking one sleekly elegant hand towards the seat next to him.

The suggestion that she was not being civilised cut her to the quick. Niesha brushed it aside. She didn't really care what his opinion was of her. All she cared about was that this evening's conversation ended with her achieving her freedom.

Nevertheless, she made her way to the sofa, acutely aware that he followed her every step until she perched on the corner of it, tucking her legs neatly to one side and folding her hands in her lap. Only then did she lift her head and meet his gaze full on. An expression passed through his eyes, gone too quickly for her to decipher.

'I'm sitting down now, Your Highness. Please explain yourself.'

He gave the barest hint of a smile, but it was gone an instant later.

'The constitution is not as backwards as I allowed you to think. Divorce isn't disallowed, but, were I to divorce, I would be the first in my family's history to do so.'

Relief surged through her, but it was accompanied by an alien, disturbing sensation she couldn't quite pinpoint. 'We can divorce?' she repeated slowly, wondering why the words attempted to stick in her throat.

He remained silent for a long moment, then he gave a brisk nod. 'Yes.' The word was uttered with a single, acrid bite. 'There is a clause that states that divorce can be initiated by either party, but there are specific circumstances under which it will be considered.'

'What circumstances?'

His nostrils flared. 'Infidelity.'

Her eyes widened when he didn't continue. 'That's it?'

'Yes,' he said.

'But—I'm not... This isn't a true marriage...not that

I have any intention of doing…being unfaithful…' She shook her head to stem her babbling. 'All this is absurd. What about an annulment?' she tagged on desperately.

He shook his head. 'No history of that in my family either.' An intensely arrogant expression crossed his face. 'No al Khalia has failed to consummate his marriage.'

For some reason that statement sent a bolt of heat surging through her belly. 'But you're going to be the first though?'

Slowly, Zufar uncrossed legs, leaned forwards and rested his elbows on his knees. 'Am I?' he drawled softly, his eyes narrowed like twin lasers on her.

Niesha's fingers trembled. She clenched them tighter. 'Of course you are. That's our only choice.'

'It is not.'

The finality of those three words shook her to her very foundations. The hairs on her nape rose chillingly as he continued to regard her steadily. 'Wh-what do you mean?'

'I mean this marriage can be real.'

'Real?' she echoed as if the word were alien to her. Perhaps it was. None of what he was saying made any sense.

'Real,' he affirmed. 'I will be your husband, and you will be my wife. You will bear my children, and you will be my Queen.'

He'd said those words to her previously. And yet Niesha's jaw still dropped to the floor.

'And…why would I want to do that?'

'Because your reward would be elevation to a position very few women will ever achieve in their lifetime.

You will have the respect of a whole kingdom and the adoration of millions.'

Something curled into a tight ball inside her. 'I'm not sure when I gave you the impressive that I wanted any of that. I don't.'

He sent her a disbelieving look as he leaned forwards even further. 'You wish to remain a chambermaid for the rest of your life?'

The lash of the question was meant to wound. And it did. She didn't need reminding that she was a nobody, with no family or even friends she could count on. That all she had was the deep yearning to leave a mark deeper and more meaningful than the sad and transient childhood that had been thrust upon her.

Despite her shredded emotions, she kicked up her chin, glared down her nose at him. 'No. I have a little bit more ambition than that. But it doesn't involve sitting around basking in the adoration of your subjects.'

He nodded, as if he hadn't all but snorted his disbelief moments before. 'Very well, tell me what it is.'

'Why?' she asked suspiciously.

He levelled a shrug so beautifully arrogant and elegant she blinked a few times before she could concentrate again. 'Perhaps I can help.'

Niesha shook her head. Nothing came for free. She knew that all too well. But his eyes were hypnotising her, the gold depths drilling to the heart of her desires.

She found herself responding before she could stop herself. 'I've always wanted to work with children,' she said softly. 'I've been saving to start a course next year.'

'A tutor will be hired for you,' he declared immediately.

Her breath caught, but the reminder that nothing came

for free stuck harder. 'In return for what? You want something, I know you do. Why don't you just tell me?'

His eyes gleamed at her. 'I have already told you.'

She shook her head, shaken beyond belief. 'This cannot possibly be what you want. You…you don't even know me.' Her voice was a perplexed shrill.

He shrugged again. 'Perhaps a blank slate is exactly what I need.' The hardness to his tone sent a cold shiver through her.

'That doesn't make any sense.'

'It may seem that way to you, little one.'

The bolt that went through her this time was all heat and charged electricity. 'Please stop calling me that.'

He stiffened. 'Does it offend you?'

She bit her lip but remained silent because, contrary to offence, every time he used that low, deep-voiced endearment, something decadent churned within her, something she didn't want to fathom, never mind explain.

Everything about this man pushed her severely off kilter. But it was time for her to regain her balance.

Before she could speak, he rose to his full, imperious height.

Long, elegant strides brought him to where she sat, and he lowered himself into the seat next to her.

The virile force of his masculinity hit her square in the face. Niesha attempted to swallow, and realised that even that small action couldn't be achieved with him so close.

'Today my people confirmed what I have known for a while—that they need the stability of a king who is married and stable rather than one who is not. The economic potential of my marriage is immense. To upset that turn of events will be unfortunate and unaccept-. able. For your part, you have been accepted into their hearts. You, a nobody from nowhere. Even if I wanted to be the first in my family to divorce, which I do not, the reaction to our union has made me rethink my decision. You will stay married to me, and in return I will give you a better life.'

Her insides shook but Niesha forced herself to speak. 'And what life is that, exactly?' She wasn't asking because she was about to accept his ludicrous proposal. She just wanted to buy herself a little time to come up with her own strategy to extricate herself from this situation.

'Any life you wish for yourself.'

'And what about Amira?'

His jaw grew rigid for one second. 'You said she wasn't coerced into leaving. Unless you were mistaken?' he asked, one eyebrow lifted.

She bit her lip, recalling those moments in the room. As much as she wanted to deny it, the truth had been plain to see. 'No, she wasn't coerced. But don't you want to find her?'

'I know exactly who took her and why. It was meant to cause humiliation and chaos, and I've successfully averted that.'

She frowned. 'But you'll want her back, surely?'

His face shuttered. 'I spoke to her father before the ceremony. Our arrangement is broken.'

'Just like that?'

He gave a cold, firm nod. 'Yes. Besides, I believe I've already said I've made my choice. Right now, I want to discuss us.'

Her heart shuddered once more. *Us.* When had they become us?

'My people have been through enough,' he continued forcefully. 'I will not jeopardise the stability of this kingdom with another emotional spectacle like the one my father exhibited recently.' The heat behind his words shocked her to the core. As if he hadn't intended those words to slip out, his face tightened. 'I need someone with a clear head and a strong work ethic by my side.'

'But…you don't even know me,' she repeated.

'I've seen your file. Spoken to those that matter. Your work in my palace has been exemplary.'

She stared at him, stunned. 'And that's it? That's all it takes?'

'No, that's not all it takes. But it's a good basis on which to start.'

Niesha shook her head, her racing heart seeming to have no intention of slowing down. 'This can't be happening,' she said under her breath.

'Reconcile yourself to it.' The finality to the words frightened her.

'I don't want to,' she whispered heatedly. 'You said this was an interim solution,' she reminded him.

Without warning, he reached out and brushed his knuckle down her cheek. The action, electrifying and unexpected, froze her in her seat.

Several minutes passed in silence. When she chanced a glance at him, his eyes were narrowed, the look in his eyes intently calculating.

Niesha was sure that whatever was going on behind his breathtaking face wouldn't include setting her free.

'My people need us to remain married, Niesha,' he eventually said.

Her heart squeezed painfully. 'I…I don't want to make them unhappy but—'

'But what? You wish to return to a life of single servitude?'

'I want to have a choice in when and who I marry!'

His hand dropped, his expression tightening in offence. 'And I'm so vastly unsuitable?'

'I didn't say that,' she mumbled. On the contrary, he was a little too close to her ideal specification of a husband.

'What will suit you, then?' he asked, but Niesha had a feeling he was just humouring her.

Her chin went up. 'For you to honour your initial agreement, that this was only temporary.'

Again he went silent for several spine-tingling minutes. Then he nodded. 'Very well. Five years,' he murmured deeply and abruptly. 'That is all I ask. Five years.'

'I… What?'

'If a permanent marriage to me is too much for you to handle, then let's revisit our situation in five years. In the meantime, you stay by my side. Bear my heirs. At the end of it, if you still want your freedom, I will grant it to you. In return, you will have the education you want, any position you desire, the title of Queen, and riches beyond your wildest dreams.'

'Can you please stop talking about your wealth? I don't want your money.'

His forefinger tucked under her chin and lifted her gaze up to meet his. 'What about my people? Do you hate them so much that you wish to see them unhappy?'

'That's not fair,' she said.

A grim smile played around his lips. 'Get your head out of the clouds, little one. If life was fair, you would not have ended up in an orphanage.'

There was no malice in his tone, only stark truthfulness. And yet the pain was hard to block out. Although there was no record of her past, the quality of the clothes on her back when she'd been found wandering dangerously close to a ravine had indicated that she might have been cared for at one point. But this was no salve right now. Well off or not, she'd been abandoned, possibly left for dead, the orphanage matron had informed her after endless probing.

Niesha had stopped asking about her past when every query—besides those about what she'd been wearing the day she was found at just five years old—had met with a stern rebuke to look forwards not backwards. She had a roof over her head and food in her belly. She needed to be grateful for that, she was told.

Nevertheless, those questions had never left her. It was what fuelled the burning need to work with children. Especially orphaned children.

If she could at some point in the future reunite one child with their rightful past that would be enough for her. Because the pain lodged in her heart all these years later wasn't something she wanted any child to experience.

The idea that Zufar al Khalia could expedite everything she'd ever dreamed of slowly wove through the waves of pain. The other things he had mentioned—being Queen, bearing his children—sent bolts of anxiety through her. They were so impossibly far-reaching she shook her head. 'You…want me to have your children?'

His lips twisted. 'That is generally the idea when a man takes a wife. But especially so in my case since mine is a hereditary rule.'

She stopped herself from laughing hysterically. Was she even capable?

'If you're wondering if you can bear children, I've also seen your medical file. There's nothing to suggest that you may not be able to carry my children.'

Was there a square inch of her life he hadn't probed? The question was ludicrous, of course. He was the head of the royal family. It stood to reason that he would cover every base. Even though they'd been brought together by a set of bizarre circumstances, it seemed as if Zufar had every intention of making this work.

But did she?

'I need your answer, little one.' He pressed his finger still resting beneath her chin, not allowing any avenue of escape.

'Children,' she echoed, her mind darting to his face, unable to stop her imagination from running wild. Would their offspring look like him? Images bombarded her, filling her with a sudden longing that robbed her of breath.

'Many,' he echoed. 'As many as we can manage in five years.'

The prospect of marriage and children had been abstract thoughts in the daily grind of her work in the palace. It was something she had hoped would happen in the future. The reality that it was happening now, unfolding right before her eyes, was almost too much to take in.

As if he knew he had her on the ropes, that she was reeling from everything he had laid out at her feet, he leaned forwards until his mouth was a scant inch from hers. 'Do you agree?' he breathed.

Marriage. Children. Everything the foolish sixteen-year-old in her had dared to dream about as she'd thumbed through the glossy pages of the royal books in the library. Those daydreams that had followed her into her sleep now wormed their way through the dazed anxiety pressing down on her.

Zufar had spoken no words of love—nor had she expected him to. But looking into the hard contours of his face, she doubted they would be forthcoming in the future. When it came right down to it, they were strangers to one another, thrown together by harsh circumstance.

Still, she couldn't dismiss that image of her sixteen-year-old self, staring after a much younger Zufar as he strode commandingly through the palace.

He'd led a life of integrity, loyalty, absolute dedication to his people; his crown. What better characteristics to look for in a future partner than those?

The notion that she was talking herself into this struck her hard.

She attempted to move, to give herself breathing room.

He stopped her retreat by slipping his hand to her nape, just as he had on the balcony earlier. Eyes sharp with intent gazed deeper into hers. 'You want this,' he murmured. 'Think about all you stand to gain, all the children you can help. Say yes, Niesha,' he pressed deeply. Hypnotically.

Had she yearned to retreat to a life of drudgery only an hour ago? Did she really want to scuttle away to her lonely bedsit and scrimp and save for years until she could make something more of her life?

She knew without a doubt that she would kick herself

from here to eternity if she refused to take the chance being offered to her on a silver platter.

His lips moved tantalisingly close, eliciting a deep craving that scandalised her. She wanted to kiss him again, she realised shockingly. Wanted the chance beyond today, beyond tomorrow, as many days as she would be granted.

With Zufar al Khalia, there would never be any doubt that her children would be nobodies like her. They would be princes and princesses, future kings or queens with centuries of history and pedigree at their fingertips. She could set a true path for her children. Perhaps even find an identity for herself that she'd been denied. Maybe that was a little bit wrong. But in that moment, it was a decision Niesha couldn't walk away from.

Her hands twisted in her lap. In the next moment, he grasped them with his free hand. He was taking control of her life, of her whole being, and she didn't even care. Her gaze dropped to the mouth she wanted to kiss so badly, before rising to meet his once again.

And then she breathed the word that seared into her heart. 'Yes.'

For endless heartbeats, he didn't move. Then, without granting her the kiss that she craved, he rose, grasped her elbow and pulled her up with him.

'You have made a wise decision,' he intoned.

'Have I, Your Highness?' she responded dazedly.

Again the corner of his mouth lifted in a barely there smile. 'You really need to stop calling me that.'

A shaky breath moved her. Then her breath stilled completely as he cupped her face in his large, warm hands. 'After all, you can hardly call me *Your Highness* when I am deep inside you,' he said in a low, thick voice.

'I...?' She stopped as heat flamed her face.

'Zufar,' he urged. 'That is my name. Use it.' His thumb caressed her jaw, rendering her speechless.

Numbly, she shook her head.

'Never fear, I will have you screaming it by the time the night is over,' he vowed deeply.

He dropped his hand and captured one wrist. The next moment he was pulling her towards the door.

'Where are you taking me?' she blurted.

'It's our wedding night, little one,' he said without breaking stride. 'Royal tradition is no different from any other. We will consummate our marriage this night. After all, if five years is all we have, then you will need to bear my children sooner rather than later, don't you think?'

The look he threw over his shoulder was filled with rock-hard purpose. There was lust in there, sure—no matter how discreet he'd been, Zufar's liaisons with beautiful women were a known fact—but it was a contained lust, one he seemed determined to keep under lock and key.

As he'd said, tonight was their wedding night. And Zufar fully intended to carry out his duty in the bedroom.

Immediately.

Heart in her throat, she stumbled after him down an endless corridor into his private bedchamber and towards the vast and solid four-poster bed that would be the venue for their wedding night.

The place where she would lose her virginity to the King of Khalia before the night was out.

CHAPTER FIVE

NIESHA BARELY ACKNOWLEDGED the magnificently appointed private suite she'd been so in awe of the handful of times she'd visited the King's bedroom as a chambermaid.

Her every sense was focused on the searing clasp of his fingers against hers. Their palms were glued together, the heat from his branding her, imprinting on her skin the same way the royal crest was embossed on the flags that fluttered along the driveway leading to the palace.

Her heart hammered loud enough to drown out any other sound in her ears, so much so that she was terrified she would hyperventilate if she didn't find a way to calm down. But how could she? How could she remain serene in the face of this earth-shaking set of events unfolding in her life?

This morning she'd woken up believing her day would be ordinary—save for the momentous event of the royal wedding, of course—but here she was on the verge of giving her virginity to the King.

Did she have to tell him? Would he know? What was the etiquette? The flurry of questions reeled through her mind, adding to the turmoil seething inside her.

As if he sensed her unsettling thoughts, Zufar stopped abruptly. 'What's wrong?'

'I... This is going too fast,' she answered truthfully.

She expected another one of his thunderous frowns, but was surprised when he studied her for a moment and then nodded. Without releasing her, he raised his other hand and gently brushed his fingers down her pale cheek. 'Do not fear, little one, I will make this memorable for you. We will endeavour to go as slow as you wish.'

A swell of relief bloomed through her apprehension. In the next moment, it all evaporated when he cleanly swept her off her feet.

'What are you doing?' she squeaked.

'I believe this is the tradition?' he replied.

He wasn't moving. He stared down steadily, waiting for an answer. Only then did Niesha realise that they were poised outside the doors to his inner bedchamber. Beyond that, the immense emperor-sized bed waited, covered with the exquisite gold and blue coverlet she herself had laid on it only a few days ago. The insane, whirlwind journey from then to now seemed like a hallucination.

A quick swallow later, she redirected her gaze to him. 'If you believe in that sort of thing, I guess,' she murmured.

One eyebrow slowly lifted. 'Do you not believe, Niesha?'

It wasn't the first time he'd said her name, but this time the effect of the deep baritone curling around her given name sent tiny bursts of fireworks from deep in her belly, radiating outwards. She watched him track her blush, a small smile curving his lips, drawing her eyes to the sensual outline of his masculine mouth.

'I believe I have my answer,' he said.

With that, he stepped over the threshold and calmly walked her over to the bed.

Slowly he set her down on her feet, his hands trailing her upper arms to settle on her shoulders. Then his gaze raked her from head to toe, lingering at her breasts and her hips in a very frank, masculine appraisal that sent a flare of awareness over her skin.

Her nipples began to pebble, her breasts growing sensitive as he lifted eyes turned molten gold to her face.

'Beautiful,' he pronounced deeply.

No one had ever called her that. Not even close. She shook her head. 'It's not me. It's the dress and…the make-up.'

'It is also the woman wearing those things,' he declared haughtily.

Recalling that he'd been responsible for the gown she was wearing, she looked down at herself. 'Thank you for this. You didn't have to but—'

He cut her off with a shake of his head. 'You were not given a choice in your wedding gown. The situation needed to be remedied for what followed. I couldn't be so distasteful to ask you to wear another woman's clothes on your wedding night.'

A knot she hadn't even been aware of eased inside her. Consideration where there needn't have been touched a place inside her that sent prickles to the back of her eyes. 'Thank you,' she said again.

'You're welcome, but I'm afraid it's time for the dress to come off.'

Just like that the atmosphere shifted again. The purposeful heat gathering in his eyes sent similar flames surging through her body. His hands slowly drifted up her shoulders to the pulse fluttering in her neck. There he paused, his fingers lazily caressing her skin until a helpless moan drifted from her throat.

'Do you like that?' he demanded, his gaze a little too incisive, as if he was intent on learning her body language.

Molten heat flashed through her. Her tongue darted out to lick dry lips as she contemplated her answer. Would he find her daring if she admitted that she liked his touch? Did she even need to answer? Surely he could see for himself?

'This is part of the "getting to know one another" process, Niesha. There's no need to be shy. I intend to learn your body, the same way I wish you to learn mine.' His elegant fingers caressed again, slightly more insistent, his touch leaving trails of heat on her skin. 'Do you like this?' he demanded again, his imperious voice setting off deep tremors inside her.

'Yes,' she moaned.

'Good.' The satisfied sound rumbled from his throat. Then, with both thumbs resting beneath her chin, he tilted her head up, exposing her face to the golden fire of his gaze. 'I wish to taste your lips again,' he stated.

Before she could stop herself, Niesha swayed towards him. A deeper satisfaction twisted his lips before his face grew taut with a captivating look from which she could not look away.

With a rough sound under his breath, he lowered his head and sealed his mouth to hers. She had no prior experience save for their previous kiss, but even Niesha knew this one was different.

For a start, it seared her to the soul. A deeply carnal, deeply intoxicating experience, it was a statement of subjugation over her that swiftly stripped her of the ability to think.

Her every sense focused on the dark magic being visited upon her, a magic she never wanted to end. The bold probe of his tongue between her lips commanded her to open up for him. With a sigh of need, she parted her lips and experienced an even greater depth of sensation as his tongue brushed hers.

Bold. Fiery. Caught in the grip of fever she'd never imagined possible with a mere kiss, she couldn't stop herself from clinging to his waist as the ground moved beneath her feet. Hungry for more, she parted her lips wider, and moaned low and deep as he explored her with brazen thoroughness. Wave after wave of sensation swept through her, her knees growing weaker with each passing second.

At some point her eyes had drifted shut as she succumbed to the power of touch and scent. She heard his breathing grow heavy to match hers, the hands resting at her throat drifting down her back to cup her buttocks before pulling her closer into his body. No man had ever touched her so boldly. No man had ever done even a fraction of what Zufar was doing to her. It was intoxicating beyond belief.

With another helpless moan, she gave into the temptation and allowed her own hands to roam his body. The silk of his tunic heated beneath her fingers as she slowly circled his waist and tentatively explored his back. Hard muscles flexed beneath her touch, his body tensing and relaxing as she hesitantly caressed him. All sense of time faded away, the only reality in her world the utterly mind-bending sensations carrying her away to an unknown destination.

A harsh hiss issued from his lips. She blinked, then realised her nails were digging into his shoulders. At some point, his fingers had buried in her hair and he used the gentle grip to notch back her head so he could gaze down into her face.

'Do I have a little hellcat on my hands?' he queried lazily.

But there was nothing lazy in his ferocious gaze. It was determined and powerful and intent on conquering.

And she wanted to be conquered. So much.

Her gaze dropped to his lips, eager and unashamed for another taste of his superb kiss.

At her moan, his eyes glittered with an indecipherable edge that escalated her heartbeat. 'You look at me with such unfettered need,' he said. 'It is enough to lead a lesser man into dangerous waters.'

'But not you,' she observed huskily.

Because he was above the weaknesses that plagued mere mortals. Even now, he stood tall and proud and domineering, statue-like evidence that he was extraordinary in every way imaginable. And so very confident in the bold manhood that branded her belly through their clothes.

Maybe it was her imagination, and she certainly had no comparison, but the imprint of his girth was substantial enough to set off a different set of alarm bells through her system.

But alongside it, there was also a thrill, sinful and delicious, temptation at its worst. Between her thighs, liquid heat threatened to melt her into a puddle, even as a terrible hunger tunnelled inside her, demanding fulfilment. She gasped as his hands slowly explored her waist, then drifted up her back once more.

Deft fingers located her zip and pulled it down with steady purpose. The sound filled the whole room a vivid manifestation of what was happening.

The noise that emerged from her this time was less of a moan and more of a whimper.

Before her nerves could eat her alive, he was wreaking havoc again, kissing one corner of her mouth before planting decadent little kisses along her cheek, her jaw and then down her neck to the point where it met her shoulder. Merciless teeth nipped at her skin, dragging a shiver that drew a deep grunt of satisfaction from him.

'You are so responsive. I look forwards to drawing even more reactions from this body.'

The soft breeze that whispered over her skin was her first indication that her dress was undone. Still kissing her neck, he slowly drew the emerald silk down her arms until her breasts were bared to his gaze.

Alarm rushed over Niesha, dampening her desire. Her arms slammed across her chest, covering her breasts as she took a hasty step back.

Zufar froze. A thunderous frown gathered on his brow. 'Something wrong?'

She swallowed hard. 'There is…something you should know.'

A faint wave of displeasure washed over his features. 'Yes?' The prompt was a tight rumble from his chest. Even as he waited for her answer, his gaze moved over her, lingering on her shoulders, the breasts she was desperately shielding from his view, down to where her dress rested low on her hips.

She would never have believed a look from a man's

eyes could evoke such cataclysmic feelings inside her. And even though Zufar seemed in complete control of his faculties, the look in his eyes rendered her mute.

But she needed to speak. She had to tell him, despite her insides shrinking at the possibilities of what he would do if he found out that she was untouched. None of them filled her with elation.

Esteemed men like Zufar preferred women who knew how to please a man. The women he'd dated before were all experienced. Sophisticated. The history books she'd scoured in the library had even contained sections on how prospective brides were tutored in the art of pleasing their husbands. She knew nothing except what she'd read in romance books years ago. And even those had sounded unrealistic.

Dejected, Niesha lowered her gaze to his shoes. Zufar had seemed aroused by their kisses, but this was far more than mere kissing. Besides, he'd done all the work and now she was terrified he would find her severely lacking.

'Speak,' he commanded, the directive firm and implacable.

'I don't… I'm not…'

'Niesha.' The dangerous edge to her name sent another skitter of alarm along her nerve endings.

She raised her head, compelled by his voice. His face was a taut, unreadable mask, but she imagined she glimpsed hunger in his eyes. That bolstered her a little.

'Tell me what worries you,' he pressed.

'I'm not…experienced,' she confessed with little more than a whisper.

A wave of decipherable emotion swept across his

face. Slowly his eyes narrowed. 'I require a better definition of inexperienced,' he replied.

'Virgin,' she blurted. 'I'm a virgin. And...I don't want to disappoint you.'

For the longest time, he stared at her, his eyes a deep bronze that saw right to her soul. When his eyes conducted a searing scrutiny from her crown to her toes, Niesha was painfully reminded that she was naked from the waist up.

'The only way you will disappoint me is if you fail to tell me how that is possible.'

Another fierce blush swept over her skin.

A sound rumbled from him. Once again he seemed fascinated by her blush, his gaze following the tide of pink as it suffused her skin. When his gaze reached her face, he stared deep into her eyes, waiting for an answer.

'I would have thought it was simple enough. I've never been with a man,' she confessed in a hushed voice.

Niesha was shocked by the naked possessiveness that lit through his eyes. A moment later it was gone, but the searing flame of it remained, heating up her blood as she stared hypnotically at him; as she watched his nostrils slowly flare in a show of frayed control before he sucked in a deep breath.

'You're twenty-five,' he breathed. 'And you've never been with a man?'

Even though she was dying to hide from his all-seeing eyes, Niesha forced herself to maintain eye contact. 'No, I have not.'

His breath punched out. A single clench rippled through his jaw before he cupped her elbows. 'Then you will be mine. Only mine.'

The ruthless, irrefutable possessiveness in those

words flattened her lungs. She was struggling to breathe when he drew her arms decisively away from her body, exposing her to his eyes. Caught in a web of sorcery he wove so effortlessly, Niesha let her arms drop, trembling before him as his eyes settled on her breasts.

Another rough sound ripped from his throat. 'You are truly exquisite.'

She couldn't have moved if her life depended on it. With his eyes and his words and his commanding stature, he captivated her. She stood trembling as he firmly tugged the gaping dress over her hips.

It dropped to her ankles. He lifted her effortlessly out of the tangle of silk and lace. She should have felt vulnerable in just her panties and heels but something about the way he looked at her body sent a thrill of power through her. Maybe he wasn't as unaffected as she'd first thought.

She had very little idea of what making love with him would fully entail, but for now something about her pleased him enough to remain before her, his eyes tracing over her skin as he leisurely explored her body.

Abruptly he swung her around to face her away from him, drawing a gasp from her as his fingers circled her waist and pulled her back into the heated column of his hard, toned body.

They stayed like that for endless seconds before he notched his head into the curve of her neck, his lips tracing over her skin. Slowly, his fingers wove into her bound hair, and began to tug out the diamond pins securing the elaborate knot. One by one he discarded them until her hair cascaded over her shoulders and down her back. 'Incredible,' he breathed again.

Between her thighs, heat built, powering up into unbearable levels as he sifted his fingers through her hair, indolently, as if he had all the time in the world. Only when he was satisfied did his hand drift over her shoulder to the slope of her chest.

Without warning he cupped one breast, his hand a warm bold caress as he gently fondled her.

At her gasp, he grazed her neck with a teasing bite, even as his fingers began to toy with her nipple. Her knees turned liquid but he easily held her up.

'Mine,' he rasped hotly in her ear.

Her soft cry gave way to a helpless whimper as he mercilessly teased her nipple, stoking relentless fire in her belly she knew wouldn't be assuaged until he gave her more, more, *more*. Fully attuned to her need, his other hand cupped her other breast, torturing both peaks with expert tugs.

In that moment, Niesha was convinced she would explode. 'Oh!'

'Does my little hellcat like this?'

Her head dropped forwards as flames of hunger singed her whole being. 'Yes,' she sobbed helplessly.

He gave a soft laugh as he continued to caress her. Behind her, she heard the rustle of clothes but feared that her senses, already overloaded with new, unbelievable sensations, would send her over the edge if she looked at him.

So, letting her imagination run wild, she conjured up what Zufar looked like. But even that fevered imagining left her breathless. Hungry.

The driving need to experience the reality of him brought her head up. But before she could turn, he was touching her again, his fingers sliding beneath the waistband of her panties and firmly pushing them over her hips. Just like her dress, they pooled around her ankles and he lifted her clear of them. Then he turned her around.

Of course, her imagination had fallen far, far short.

Magnificent.

Bronzed from head to toe, there wasn't an ounce of fat on his sleek, muscled body. He could have been hewn from marble blessed by the gods themselves, he couldn't have been more perfect. The hard, hairless planes of his chest were woven into a tight six-pack, before arrowing into defined silky hair that framed an impressive manhood that jutted proudly from his body.

Niesha's jaw dropped. He was beyond impressive. So much so her body flamed with a new, intensely searing hunger as her gaze drifted down his powerful thighs to his feet and back again to that place between his legs that she couldn't pull her fascinated gaze from.

'You like what you see, little one?' he enquired with more than a touch of male arrogance.

Even as the question dropped from his lips, his manhood continued to swell. She watched, her breath completely locked in her lungs. There was no way he could fit inside her.

Accurately deciphering her thoughts, he stepped forwards. 'You needn't worry. I'll take care of you, *habibti.*'

He gave her no time to dwell on what was coming. Powerful arms swept her off her feet, laid her down on the bed and he levered himself over her. Then, excruciatingly slowly, he lowered himself until his hard chest brushed against her sensitive nipples.

At her wild tremor, one corner of his mouth lifted. The wildness intensified when he dropped down and sealed another kiss on her lips, while his hands roamed freely, possessively over her body, leaving no part of her skin untouched as he explored her thoroughly.

Niesha had no idea how much time passed before he began kissing his way down her body.

Sensual lips trailed from her collarbone to the valley between her breasts, dropping torrid, open-mouthed kisses on her skin before cupping her breasts and fondling her. Hot murmured words she couldn't decipher dripped from his lips before he captured one tight peak in this mouth.

A tiny scream tore free from her throat, her back arching off the bed as sensation like she'd never known rippled through her body. He rolled his tongue over her nipple, sucking her deep into his mouth before releasing her, only to start the torture all over again. He repeated the gesture on the twin peak, leaving her delirious and whimpering when he freed her to trail kisses over the skin above her belly button.

'Be calm,' he ordered thickly. 'You have my promise we will do this again. For now, I must taste what is mine.'

When she fully grasped his meaning, Niesha gasped, and attempted to close her legs. Surely he didn't mean…?

'Yes,' he insisted gruffly.

Powerful hands held her easily captive, clamped on her thighs as he slowly, insistently laid her bare.

His gaze snagged hers for a moment, and then his eyes dropped to her most intimate place. The fiercest, wildest blush she'd ever experienced threatened to swallow her whole as a deep rumble emitted from Zufar's throat.

'Truly exquisite.'

Niesha was spinning at the power of those two

words when his head dropped and he slicked an expert tongue over her needy flesh. A long moan ripped free. She shuddered wildly, even as every cell in her body clamoured for more. Zufar delivered, leisurely exploring her as if he owned every inch of her.

Which he did, she thought dazedly.

At some point, Niesha stopped blushing, the blissful sensation of what he was doing to her overcoming embarrassment as she gave herself over to the magic of his tongue. He teased, nibbled, explored, and then concentrated with single-minded focus on that bundle of nerves at the top of her sex.

Just when she thought there could be no sensation as thrilling as this, he suckled her with steady pressure that detonated a volcano deep in her pelvis.

She cried out, her whole body tightening for one soul-shaking instant before her world erupted in a billion fragments. Convulsions tore through her as bliss blinded her. An eternity passed. Or it might have been one enchanted minute. Niesha had no idea of the passage of time as she was fully engulfed in pure sensation.

Gradually she became aware that her fingers were curled into Zufar's hair, holding on tight as the world slowly began to right itself. She was also aware that his breathing was uneven as he trailed kisses against her skin.

It occurred to her that, far from the tightly controlled man who'd carried her into his bedroom, Zufar's demeanour had altered. He was just as caught up in the fever as she was.

And he'd been that way from the moment she'd mentioned her virginity. Or was she reading too much into it?

She had no time to dwell on it because he was kissing

his way back up her body. When they were face to face, he lowered himself onto his elbows, stared deeply into her eyes for a moment before he fused his mouth to hers. The taste of her on his lips should have embarrassed Niesha. But all it produced was a decadent triumph.

She'd done something right. He wasn't pulling away. He didn't look disappointed.

If anything, there was an edge to his kiss, an aggression that spoke to a need that matched the one rekindling inside her.

When the need to replenish their breaths forced them apart, his fevered eyes seized hers. 'Touch me,' he commanded gruffly.

Her hands trembled wildly, from the strength of her release, and from the nerves that were resurfacing. But the need to feel the warmth of his skin beneath her fingers overcame the nerves.

Just as he'd done to her, she drifted her fingers down his neck. Over his Adam's apple. His tight swallow and groan told her he liked it. Emboldened, she continued to touch him, caressing the hard muscle of his pecs before trailing her hands down his stomach to settle on his hips.

Zufar's breathing turned harsh and uneven. With not quite steady hands, he pulled her thighs apart and settled between them. His thick length settled between her folds. Her very wet, very needy folds.

As another wave of embarrassment hit her cheeks, he smiled down at her. 'Do not be embarrassed by your eagerness for me,' he murmured. 'Spread your legs wider,' he commanded.

She complied, her heart pumping like a runaway racehorse. The broad head of his manhood nudged her flesh and Niesha's breath strangled in her throat.

'Be calm,' he instructed again.

She forced herself to breathe even as her fingers bit into the hard muscles of his arms.

Zufar inhaled sharply then pushed inside her.

The sharp pain took her completely by surprise. She cried out.

He kissed her, hard and swift. 'Hush,' he soothed gruffly. He withdrew slowly, then pushed inside her again.

Hot tears welled in her eyes as pain rippled through her again.

Above her, Zufar's jaw clenched tight, his breathing ragged as he stared down at her with dark, ferocious eyes. 'The pain will ease.' It was a directive, as if he had power over her pain too.

For some absurd reason, she believed him. And gave a jerky little nod.

As if that action had triggered something inside him, he gave a rough groan and penetrated her to the hilt. Another shaky cry tore free as tears slid down her temples. And then just as abruptly as it had arrived, the pain disappeared.

'Tell me how you feel,' he rasped.

'I…I'm fine,' she replied softly, and then realised she was.

Above her, he continued to watch her with hawk-like intensity, dark gold eyes scrutinising every expression. After a moment, he drew back, and pushed back in.

Niesha gasped at the new sensations dancing through her bloodstream. With shallow thrusts, Zufar possessed her, his eyes watching her every move as he joined their bodies.

Her moans fusing into one litany of need, she shut her eyes when Zufar lowered himself over her. His breath washed over her face as he lengthened his thrusts, drawing even more exquisite pleasure from her body.

'Wrap your legs around me,' he instructed.

An instant after she obeyed, she gasped as his next thrust drew a sharper, more intense sensation from her. With a grunt of carnal satisfaction, he fused his mouth to hers in a bold mimic of what was happening below.

Dear heaven, she'd had no idea it could be this incredible. The thought barely registered before another charge lanced through her, sending her spinning even higher.

'Oh… Zufar…'

As if his name on her lips had triggered madness inside him, his thrust grew wilder, pushing her relentlessly towards a pinnacle that far surpassed the one she'd crested only minutes ago.

Her world began to tilt again.

'Niesha, open your eyes,' he demanded.

She pried her eyes open to meet with burnished gold ones. Something about that sizzling connection was enough to send her over the edge.

With a strangled scream, she tumbled from the highest peak of sensation, falling into a never-ending sea of bliss that drew tears to her eyes.

Zufar al Khalia couldn't believe the woman beneath him was the same person he'd met only this morning; the woman he'd dismissed so carelessly. He'd gone into this believing he had his eyes wide open to every angle. Not for one single moment had he believed enjoyment would come into the undertaking. But here he was, unable to deny the surfeit of pleasure rippling through his body. He'd bedded many women in his life, but none came close to the responsiveness of his new wife.

His virgin Queen.

He wondered if it was her complete innocence that added to the thrill of the conquest. More than likely, he concluded. He'd never bedded a virgin, never felt inclined to be the first to stake a claim on a woman. To be honest, the thought of tutoring one to please him had been a deterrent rather than a draw.

But as he thrust into his new wife, Zufar thought of all the ways he could mould her to his liking. How he could teach her to take pleasure in her own body, even as he planted his seed in her womb. They were archaic, primitive thoughts that should have shamed him, but only intensified his pleasure as he let the sounds of her pleasure fill him up. She was his in every way. He stared down at her as her sweet lips parted on another pleasurable gasp, her beautiful eyes glazing over as he crested his own pinnacle.

With a raw shout, he let the sweet taste of nirvana sweep through his body.

It was only as he came down from the unparalleled high that the full effect of his thoughts began to settle in.

Shock ripped through him when he recognised how quickly he'd let temptation sway him from his purpose.

How quickly, like his father, he'd been prepared to set aside his priorities to succumb to desire.

How, for a handful of heartbeats, he'd completely lost sight of just how affairs of the flesh had ripped his family apart.

CHAPTER SIX

So THIS WAS what true desire felt like. This endless cyclone of sensation. This exceptional feeling of touching heaven.

This—

Niesha's thoughts ceased abruptly as Zufar wrenched free from the arms she hadn't even realised were locked around his shoulders, anchoring her to the present.

The thought that she'd been clinging to him like a limpet doused her with a wave of chagrin. Luckily, he wasn't looking at her. In fact, his whole body was turned away from her, and he was getting out of bed.

Heart still racing a little wildly, she watched him walk, gloriously naked and arrogantly assured in his own skin, away from the bed. But there was tension in his broad shoulders and back that chilled her with each step he took away from her. Her heart rate slowed, a little of that magic leaching from her, then fading completely as he firmly shut the bathroom door behind him.

Okay, what had happened?

She hadn't said anything. Had she done something to provoke that reaction? Minutes ago, he'd seemed… into it. Even now, the animalistic roar of his release echoed in her ears, making her blush anew at the memory. Niesha would have felt ashamed at the throb of feminine power she'd experienced in that moment, if she weren't overcome by his masculine beauty.

But that was ten minutes and a lifetime ago. The aftermath was turning out to be a different story.

Her thoughts ceased abruptly when the door opened and he strode back to the bed. She was so busy searching his expression, she didn't read his intent until he scooped her up.

'Wh-what are you doing?' she squeaked.

His eyes had grown remote, if still a touch darker than usual. They met hers for a split second before he strode, set-faced, towards the bathroom.

'Seeing to your comfort. You must be sore.' The matter-of-fact tone of his reply killed any softness the words evoked, although his touch, when he set her down in the shower cubicle and began to wash her, was gentle.

Why?

The question stayed locked in her throat as her breath shuddered out at his disturbingly intimate cleansing of her body. Niesha withstood his touch even though she wanted to sprint back into the bedroom and draw the covers over her head. It would solve nothing. So she stood there, biting her lip as he took his time to perform his task. Maybe it was no big deal. Maybe he did this for all his—

No. Not going there, she concluded fiercely.

Inexorably, her eyes rose to his face. To the tight mask blocking his every expression from her.

'Is…is everything okay?' She hated herself for seeking the reassurance.

His expression didn't change but she saw his shoulders tighten. 'Everything is fine.'

Tell that to your clenched jaw, she wanted to blurt. She bit back the words before they spilled free.

Maybe this was post-coital etiquette? Even as she pondered the question, Niesha knew she was grasping at straws. She wanted to find an excuse for the hollow sensation widening inside her but, really, wasn't it her own foolish whims leading her astray, again?

As the thought struck she noticed his movements had slowed, his hands gliding fluidly over her flesh. Breath snagging, her gaze flew to his face. His lips were parted, his tongue resting on his lip as he glided a soapy palm over her breasts. Between his thighs, his manhood was stirring into life again. Niesha's senses thrilled anew, the foolish notion that she'd got it wrong almost making her laugh with relief.

In the next moment, Zufar turned away. With almost cruel movements, he turned off the shower and stepped out of the cubicle.

No. She wasn't wrong. She'd fooled herself into thinking she'd pleased him. That he would want her again. But as he'd told her in the living room, he needed heirs—and lots of them, quickly—if they were to be married for only five years.

The need to consummate this marriage had been an essential part of that goal. It had had nothing to do with her. The future of the kingdom depended on it. Nothing more, nothing less.

Zufar was a man who placed his duty above all else. He'd performed it and now the act was over.

Despite the warmth of the shower, a chill settled over her. Growing stiffer by the minute, she concentrated on breathing in and out as he wrapped a towel around himself, then one around her, before carrying her back to the bedroom.

Immediately she fled to the far side of the bed. Then, wondering if she was sleeping on his side, she started to reverse position. Then froze in the middle when it occurred to her that they hadn't even discussed sleeping arrangements.

Niesha knew that besides the previous Queen's private suite in the east wing, there was an adjoining suite next to the King's for the Queen's use. Was she supposed to retire there now and await further summons or return to the east wing? Her hands curling in frustration, she started to move to the edge of the bed.

'Where are you going?' he drawled, his imposing figure looming beside her.

A furtive gaze confirmed his demeanour hadn't changed. In fact, he looked even more remote. 'I don't know which side you preferred or…even if I'm supposed to sleep here?'

His brows gathered in a dark frown. 'Where else are you supposed to sleep?'

She licked her lips, her fingers tightening on the sheets bunched between her breasts. 'In the suite next door? Or back in the Qu… Queen's quarters?' She stumbled over the word, was positive she would stumble over it for a long time to come.

His face darkened further, his jaw jutting out as he stared down his patrician nose at her. 'Is that what you would prefer?' he asked with chilling terseness.

Niesha suppressed a shiver. At this moment, she would prefer to be anywhere but here, withstanding his cold, haughty scrutiny, which he managed to pull off superbly despite being completely naked. 'Isn't that what is expected of me?'

'What would make you draw that conclusion?' he bit out.

'It wasn't a secret that your parents did not share the same bed...' Her words withered to nothing when his whole body clenched into terrifying stillness.

'In case the obvious needs pointing out, I'm not my father. And this is not the nineteenth century.' If she'd thought him remote a minute ago, he was positively arctic now.

For some reason, mentioning his parents had hit the wrong nerve. Niesha, like everyone else living within the palace walls, had heard whispers of the strained relationship between the previous King and his wife, despite the King's utter devotion to her. But with no facts to back it up, she'd attributed it to palace gossip. As for the relationship between King Tariq and his children, it had appeared civil if not outwardly warm.

But from Zufar's reaction...could it all have been an act? A series of royal chess moves designed to fool the general public?

Niesha had certainly witnessed how ruthlessly calculating her new husband could be when he desired a specific outcome. Her current position was the living embodiment of that ruthlessness.

She strove to speak despite the unease flaring through her body. 'I know that...but we both know this isn't a real marriage.'

Sensual lips that had kissed hers only a short while ago twisted in faint derision. 'I've just taken your virginity, Niesha. We have agreed to have children. It doesn't get more real than that,' he pointed out, his voice deeply husky and painfully direct.

Her chin dropped, every skin cell flaming. 'You know what I mean.'

'Do I?'

Her head reared up. 'Yes!' She lifted her hand to her slightly throbbing head and pushed back the heavy curtain of hair. 'Look, we both know I wasn't your first choice. I wasn't even in the running.' If Amira hadn't been seduced by another man she would be here right now. The thought lodged a hard knot in her stomach, but she pushed it away. 'So it's completely understandable if you want to maintain your private quarters.'

He took a step closer, braced one knee on the bed. It took everything in her power not to drop her gaze to the impressive manhood between his legs. A part of her felt bitter jealousy for his ability to be so confident in his own skin, especially when she couldn't even control her own stupid blushes.

Her breath stilled as firm hands captured her chin.

'I ask again, is that what you want?' Piercing eyes probed hers.

He seemed to be fishing for something specific. Something she had no clue about. She blinked, glanced at the tousled bed. Unbidden, the image of going to sleep in the same bed as Zufar, surrounded by his unique scent, his magnificent body, the sizzling mastery of his possession, and waking up with him, loomed in her mind.

Did she want that?

Not if each one ended with him staring at her with such remote, almost indifferent eyes. But then how else would she live up to her end of the bargain? Surely it was better to remain here, ensure the deed was done in the shortest possible time?

'As you said, the quicker we ensure that I'm… pregnant, the better for everyone, I think—' The words stuck in her throat, most likely because they were far too clinical, stripped of any emotion, and it wasn't a true reflection of what was happening inside her.

But he was nodding, as if in complete agreement with her.

It drove home the fact that she couldn't afford to let her emotions run free. Or give into foolish dreams of this union being anything but the stark bargain she'd struck. She was only here because another man had stolen the woman he'd chosen.

As for hoping her child was conceived in contentment and warmth, it was really past time she put those fairy-tale notions behind her. Not when she was the epitome of what came *after* conception.

Abandonment. Loneliness. Deprivation.

All things she needed to ensure never happened to her child, no matter how it was conceived.

He dropped her chin and slid into bed. 'I'm glad to hear it. And for the record, this is what I prefer, too. Tomorrow the palace designer will contact your assistant with a view to setting up a meeting.'

'What for?' she asked.

'To discuss what you intend to do with the suite next door. You can turn it into a giant dressing room. Or perhaps a nursery. Entirely up to you.'

Niesha was grappling with that when he pulled the sheets from her with a firm tug and began to rearrange the covers over them.

'You've had a challenging day. Tomorrow will not be any less so. I suggest you get some sleep now.'

On that none-too-reassuring pronouncement, he turned away and doused the bedside lamps.

Niesha awoke to the breath-stealing sensation of a stubbled jaw grazing her cheek. Still lost in a jagged dream of smoke and fire and screams, it was a relief to awaken.

It wasn't the first time she'd had those dreams. Along with the soft voice that echoed reassurance in her mind in times of distress, the disturbing dreams had also been part of her life for as long as she could remember.

It wasn't a stretch to conclude it was her psyche grappling with whatever dark shadows lurked in her past. That the thoughts and fears she pushed to the back of her mind during her waking hours transmitted to nightmares in her sleep.

Despite knowing this, she still woke most mornings with a panicked, racing heart and a sinking sensation that her past would always remain a pitch-black, desolate landscape to her.

Not this morning, though. Before her anxiety could take hold, firm masculine lips moved along her jawline to the corner of hers.

She shuddered, then opened her eyes to meet dark gold ones that burned with single-minded purpose. For the longest moment, Zufar stared at her. He didn't utter a word. Neither did she.

Then one hand dipped between their bodies to settle firmly between her thighs. At her gasp, his nostrils flared, the only sign that he'd registered her response.

The moment he established that she was wet, needy

and more than ready for him, he angled the thick column of his erection and thrust, deeply and powerfully, inside her.

Her husky moan was filled with need and awe, her senses ripping apart at the potency of his possession.

Even when she realised that the only sounds filling the room were coming from her, his silent lovemaking was still electrifying, perhaps even more so than the night before since her body now knew what to expect.

Minutes later, she found out that even in that she was wrong, that there was a new determination in his lovemaking that robbed her of the little breath she'd managed to sustain.

He captured and pinned her arms above her head, and then, with caged intensity, he thrust relentlessly into her, the formidable power of it driving home one purpose—ensuring she took his seed and produced the heir he wanted.

The small part of her that attempted to shrink back from such a complete but detached coupling was soon swept under the traitorous melting that radiated from her core and took control of her own being.

The tiny cry she gave as she crested the pinnacle of pleasure was soon followed by his suppressed groan as he, too, achieved his release.

Moments later, he left the bed. She heard the muted hiss of the shower and sagged onto the pillows, willing her heartbeat and the tumultuous emotions reeling through her to slow.

She really couldn't afford to lose her mind each time he touched her. Every instinct warned that would be reckless in the extreme. Already his brief absence was triggering a craving for another glimpse of him, and somewhere in the back of her mind a tiny clock was counting down the five years she'd agreed with him.

What would happen afterwards?

Banishment from the palace? Niesha jackknifed into sitting position, realising she should have hammered out more than just parting with her freedom for five years. Would she be allowed to take her children with her? Or would she be once again condemned to a life of loneliness and desolation?

She firmed her lips. No, she wouldn't let that happen. No matter what, the children she produced with Zufar would be part hers.

But then he was the King, with endless resources to fight her if he so wished.

She was grappling with the future threat when he emerged from the bathroom. And just like that every thought evaporated from her head.

His thick black hair was slicked back from his face, glistening damply beneath the low-lit chandeliers. His arms and chest rippled with sleek muscles as he strode towards the bed. But it was the snowy white towel, knotted low on his hips and framing the divine V of his pelvis, that made her mouth water shamefully.

She held her breath, unable to prise her gaze from him as he sauntered over to the bed.

A moment passed, then two. At his continued silent scrutiny, she dragged her head up. 'Good morning,' she said after swallowing hard.

He raised an eyebrow. 'Is it?'

Her fingers bunched in the sheets, her heart lurching wildly. Had the new day triggered a change of mind? Did he wish to renege on the deal he'd struck? Was he going to chase after Amira after all?

Why that thought left a pile of ash in her mouth when she'd all but demanded the very same thing last night floored her.

She lifted a hand in a futile attempt to ease the sudden sharp ache hammering beneath her breastbone.

'I ask because you were having a distressing dream. It was why I woke you up.'

Her hand dropped to her lap, unsettling relief weaving through her. A moment later, her heart dropped too, slowing to a disturbingly dull thud. Was that why he'd made love to her too? To distract her from her nightmare?

'Oh, I see. Thank you,' she murmured, because, really, what did it matter why he'd woken her? She'd agreed, without force or coercion, to be his brood mare. So why was the reality dampening her mood?

His eyes narrowed on her face. 'Are you well?' he asked abruptly.

Did he mean the nightmare? Or what had happened last night and this morning. Or generally? Again, what did it matter? She nodded jerkily. 'I...I'm fine.'

He gave a brisk nod. 'You will join me for breakfast. After that, your time is your own, save for the hour or so you need to select your staff. My chief aide will provide you with a shortlist.'

The briskness with which he walked away towards his dressing room told her she didn't have time to linger on yet another bombshell dropped so neatly at her feet. She would think about what on earth she would do with a staff later, when she was appropriately dressed.

As she rose from the bed, she spotted the telltale signs of her lost virginity on the sheets and her face flamed all over again. Glad Zufar wasn't around to spot her embarrassment, Niesha located her discarded dress and fled the room before he could return.

Her walk of shame wasn't any less cringe-inducing because she was the Sheikh's new bride, because of course the palace was wide awake and the usual bustle of people that went into making the place run like a well-oiled machine were up and about. Her state wasn't helped when her attendants, headed by Halimah, who looked as if they'd been lying in wait for her, descended on her the moment she entered the main wing of the palace.

Within minutes everyone knew she'd spent the night in Zufar's bed.

Niesha managed to hold her head high as she was escorted back to her rooms.

Again, a stunning array of clothes had been hung out for her, this time lighter linens and soft chiffons in pastel colours. Unsure how long she had before her breakfast with Zufar, she declined having her hair washed and didn't linger in the bath.

Twenty minutes later, dressed in a knee-length ivory and navy block dress with a delicate lace waistline fringe, capped sleeves, and navy platform heels, she retraced her steps back to Zufar's private quarters. An aide led her into the dining room, where he sat at the head of a long antique dining table, reading a newspaper.

Even performing the mundane task of reading while he ate, he was a spectacular sight, dressed in an impeccable suit she knew had been specially imported from Milan.

When she neared him, he deftly folded the paper, inclined his head in a regal nod and watched as she was seated. She kept her hands folded in her lap and her spine straight, tinglingly aware of his direct gaze as her tea was poured and various dishes placed before her.

'You left my bed before I could show you the less… public passage from my room,' he said with a stiffness that spoke of his displeasure the moment the staff retreated.

Niesha fought the blush that threatened. 'Oh…I… didn't know—'

He waved her response away. 'It is done. And since you won't need to leave my bedroom again in the future, we will not speak about your precipitous exit. Eat your breakfast.'

Niesha stared down at her plate, trying to summon an appetite, while curbing a bite of irritation. Slowly she reached for a piece of toast, buttered it and added a dollop of jam made from dates and honey. It melted on her tongue, but, where she would probably have groaned with the delicious taste, she chewed thoughtfully.

'Something wrong?' he queried after a minute.

'You made it sound as if I needed your permission to leave.'

His gaze scoured her face. 'Or perhaps I wished to spare the blushes that come so readily to your cheeks,' he retorted.

It took great effort not to lift her hands to her hot face. 'I'm sorry if my comportment is lacking.'

Something flashed in his eyes before they regained that remoteness again. 'On the contrary, you're the epitome of a blushing bride. Legions of people across the world lap up that sort of thing, I'm told,' he said lazily.

She barely managed to stop herself from asking who'd told him. Did she really want to know who he'd been discussing her with? Or whether he had an opinion on blushes one way or the other?

But even as she thought that, she felt his gaze tracking another rush of heat to her face. One day she would master her flaw. Today she had other matters on her mind.

'What you said yesterday, about the honeymoon… Is it still happening?'

Steady eyes rested on her. 'Of course. Why should it not be?'

Because he'd planned it for another woman. Under the circumstances, the idea shouldn't have lodged a tiny stone beneath her breastbone but she couldn't forestall the ache. She shook her head. 'I was just double-checking.'

'If you're feeling a little…bruised because I'm taking you where I would've taken Amira, don't be. Like you, she and I had an understanding. The continued prosperity and smooth running of the kingdom comes first. Which is why this trip was always going to be partly a business one.'

She wasn't sure whether knowing she was so interchangeable made her feel better or worse. Or that he wasn't bothering to soften where his priorities truly lay. 'When do we leave?' she asked when she'd smothered the growing hurt in her chest.

'In three days. We will stay at the Emerald Palace for two days, then leave for Europe.'

He went on to name the other places they would be visiting, places Niesha had dreamed of exploring once upon a time. But the joy she'd felt then was severely lacking now. She finished sipping her tea, nodding when expected, all the while feeling the cloak of loneliness and abandonment encroaching once more.

Would she ever be rid of this feeling? She was tied

to one of the most powerful men in the world, and yet she felt…hollow.

'I seem to have lost you.' His hard, abrupt observation prised her from her thoughts.

Before she could respond, a knock rapped on the dining-room doors. An instant later, a ping sounded on his phone. He touched the screen as the door opened, and his private secretary strode in.

'Good morning, Your Highnesses,' he greeted, bowing low before turning to Zufar. 'You are needed urgently, sire.' He didn't say more, but whatever lay behind his words was enough to make Zufar's face tighten.

Without further questioning, he rose from the table. 'I'm afraid I need to start my day earlier than planned. Finish your breakfast. Your aide will be here in half an hour.'

With that, he swept out with all the regal authority and purpose of a true king.

Niesha deflated the moment she was alone. After a few minutes of toying with the fresh fruit on her plate, she rose and went to the window. Outside the sun was blazing. On the palace grounds, the remaining signs of the wedding were being removed. In a few hours, it would be a thing of the past.

Desolation crept closer, wrapping tighter around her.

She realised that somewhere between last night and this morning, she'd let the tiniest grain of hope take root, fooled herself into thinking that the bargain she'd struck with Zufar would immediately go towards filling the yawning hole she'd felt all these years.

But it still gaped as wide as ever.

A throat cleared behind her and she steeled herself not to stiffen.

'Your Highness?'

She turned. The woman dressed in a sharp skirt suit was tall, statuesque, with kind brown eyes and an easy, deferential smile. 'My name is Kadira Hamdi and I'm your new aide.'

Niesha had never seen her before but something about her expression eased the knot inside her. For starters, there was none of the judgement in her eyes that she'd witnessed in Halimah's.

And even though the woman before her was stunningly beautiful, Niesha sensed no malice in her.

She nodded and returned the smile. 'I'm Niesha… but of course you know that…' She trailed off, feeling a little out of sorts. She smothered her unsettled emotions. 'What's on my agenda this morning?' she asked brightly.

Kadira stepped forwards, opened a leather-bound folder and ran her finger down a long list of items. 'We will do as much or as little as you desire, Your Highness, but I suggest we get your honeymoon wardrobe squared away. With your permission, I'll have the three stylists I have on standby meet with us now?'

Niesha tried to hide her nervous gulp with a smile. 'That works for me.'

Kadira's smile widened, before she reached for the phone tucked into her folder. Her fingers flew over the surface for a few seconds. 'If you're ready, Your Highness,' she said with a graceful dip of her head.

Niesha left the dining room, thinking she was headed back to the women's quarters. But Kadira turned down a different hallway, one that led past many doors and into Zufar's private suite.

On entering, Niesha realised it was the one that connected the previous Queen's rooms to Zufar's, the one he'd suggested she turn into a dressing room or nursery. She barely had the time to take in the fact that the previously fully furnished room was now empty before Kadira was leading her through a narrow hallway into another room.

This one was just off Zufar's bedroom and was a dressing room similar to his. Within the space large enough to hold an entire new suite, sumptuous sofas had been set up against one wall, with half of the closet space already filled with designer labels and accessories.

'Whose clothes are these?' she asked, a little more sharply than intended.

Kadira looked surprised. 'They're yours, Your Highness. His Highness instructed your belongings to be moved here this morning.'

Niesha hid her surprise at how quickly Zufar had acted, took a seat, then focused as Kadira continued, 'The rest of the space will be filled according to the seasons once the designers have made their presentations.'

'I understand,' Niesha murmured.

Moments later, the stylists arrived, trailing assistants pushing endless clothes rails.

For the next two hours she was bombarded with choices and suggestions until her head started to throb.

The sheer scale of opulence was staggering, and Niesha was glad she was sitting down. She knew another woman in her shoes would have jumped for joy at being so totally immersed in wealth and privilege but, in that moment, she would have given all of it away for a crumb of her past, because she knew that even dressing in the most luxurious clothes and jewels wouldn't dull the persistent ache in her heart.

She was about to ask for a reprieve, or a cup of tea, when a sharply voiced command preceded Zufar's majestic entrance into the room. Everyone stilled for a second, before executing a curtsey, which he acknowledged with a sweep of his hand.

'Leave us.' The command was brusque.

The room emptied in seconds. For a full minute he didn't speak, just paced in a tight, inflexible line that spoke of his military training.

'Is…is something wrong?' she asked, after watching his jaw clench a few times.

He stopped abruptly and looked at her. 'Yes, we'll have to postpone the honeymoon.' The tightness behind his words drew unease but it was the way he loosened his tie a moment later that caught her attention.

She'd never seen Zufar even a little bit dishevelled, and that included the moment he had found out his betrothed had disappeared through a window only hours before they had been due to wed. Now she watched as he released the first two buttons of his shirt with an angry flick of his elegant hands.

'Oh?'

'Only by a few days, perhaps a week.'

'May I ask why?'

He exhaled harshly. 'It seems one scandal in twenty-four hours isn't enough for my family,' he said by way of explanation. Ice-cold anger bathed his words and she watched, utterly fascinated, as he clawed a hand through his dark hair, upsetting its usually neat order.

He paced to the end of the room and abruptly reversed course.

Was it something to do with Amira? Unable to stand the suspense, she spoke. 'Zufar…'

He froze, his eyes meeting hers across the wide space at her use of his name.

Nervous at the intensity of his gaze and the unsettling need to ease his angst, she slicked her tongue over her upper lip and plunged ahead. 'Can…can I help?'

Surprise flickered over his face even as his gaze lowered to lock on her mouth. After a moment, he lifted his head.

'I'm being blackmailed,' he pronounced icily.

She gasped. 'What? Is it about Amira?' she forced herself to ask.

He frowned, then his jaw rippled. 'No. It looks like her choice was definitive. I've seen security footage of her leaving the palace, which confirms she went of her own free will. I will no longer be wasting time and attention on her.'

The cold dismissal sent tremors through her, probably because of the quiet fury that lingered in his voice when he spoke of her. Perhaps he wouldn't take her back but he wasn't as unaffected as his words suggested.

'Unfortunately, the new set of issues involves my sister.'

Niesha refocused, and frowned. 'Princess Galila? What did she do? Is she okay?'

Zufar exhaled another breath full of ire. 'She's in the middle of what can politely be termed as a hissy fit. One she's blindly refusing to admit is the result of her own actions.' He started pacing again. 'Apparently, she saw fit to get blind drunk at the wedding reception and let loose a few family secrets to a complete stranger,' he snarled as he reached the far wall of the dressing room and reversed direction.

'What secrets?'

Zufar eyed her with narrow-eyed ferocity. About to pre-empt a response to mind her own business, she swallowed her words as he slowly advanced to tower over her. He seemed to be weighing his options. After a moment, his fist unfurled and he lowered his formidable length into the sofa next to her.

'You're part of this family now. If this gets out it will be better that you are armed with a response rather than caught off guard.'

It hurt a little to know the only reason he was confiding in her was because he didn't trust her to react properly in public.

But then she reminded herself that she was barely twenty-four hours into this marriage. To Zufar al Khalia she was little more than a stranger thrust into his life by exceptional circumstances.

Niesha composed a nod, her spine straightening as she returned his gaze. 'Very well.'

She waited.

For several heartbeats he assessed her. Then, 'She revealed that our mother had an affair with Sheikh Karim's father over three decades ago.' He took a deep, hissing breath. 'That the affair bore a son. The same son who took Amira yesterday. So Karim not only knows my family's secrets, but he's been made aware of the existence of his half-brother.'

Niesha's jaw dropped, then her heart dropped lower. 'What?'

He didn't respond, letting the shock waves sink in.

She wasn't aware how protectively she'd held the

bubble of a happy-ever-after dream until Zufar callously burst it with his words. The royal family she'd spun her teenage dreams around was nothing more than a broken façade.

But…it was a façade that was affording her a glimpse of the not quite perfect humanity behind the thick veil.

Like her…

Niesha wasn't certain why that thought settled deep inside her. Surely she wasn't comparing herself to them? Her past was broken too, and had plenty of missing chunks. And yet she couldn't dismiss that seed of kinship taking root inside her.

'So your half-brother stole your fiancée?' she murmured, shocked.

Anger darkened his eyes, right before a low, bitter laugh emitted from his throat. 'Because he believes my position in this family should be his.'

'That's what the note meant by *birthright*?' Was that why Zufar had wanted to win the skirmish yesterday at all costs? The thought drew another cold tremor through her.

'Yes. And I believe it was a move I neatly countered and even bettered,' he said with throbbing satisfaction, confirming her suspicion.

Had she, and to some extent Amira, been perfect pawns in their game? Niesha was thankful that too many emotions swirled through her for the statement to pierce any harder. Instead she focused on the reason behind his initial anger. 'So what does this blackmailer want? Money?'

Zufar's head went back as if the reminder greatly vexed him. Which it did, if the harsh breath he expelled was an indication. 'Would that it were so. Sheikh Karim of Zyria has enough of that for it not to be his goal. He's after something else entirely.'

Niesha swallowed a gasp. The kingdom of Zyria was Khalia's direct neighbour, with shared borders and a long history of shared traditions. The magnitude of Zufar's mother's betrayal expanded in Niesha's mind. A few things began to make sense, like the haggard pain she'd glimpsed in King Tariq's face over the years.

'Your father knew, didn't he?' she asked.

After a moment, Zufar nodded. 'Yes.'

The confirmation only further shattered her rose-coloured glasses. But on the flip side, she felt a little closer to Zufar even though she knew such a feeling would only ever be one-sided.

'So if Sheikh Karim doesn't want money, what does he want?'

Zufar's jaw clenched tight until the vibrating muscle turned white. 'He wants my sister's hand in marriage. Immediately.'

Her hand flew to her mouth. 'And are you going to give your blessing?'

He shrugged. 'I have limited options. Scandal must be avoided at all costs. At least if they pull it off, my people will be happy. Two weddings within weeks of one another? Anyone would think heaven itself was smiling down on us,' he mocked bitterly.

Her heart twisted, but she clung to her composure. 'And will Galila agree?'

'She will if she wants what's best for the family,' he said curtly.

Silence descended, and then she cleared her throat. 'Can I do anything?'

Again he seemed surprised by her offer. One corner

of his mouth lifted, but any trace of mirth was wiped clean an instant later. 'A guarantee that I'll have peace for at least twenty-four hours would be greatly welcome,' he breathed.

This close, his scent wrapped around her, triggering a yearning to move closer, to feel the heat of his skin against hers. Then she reminded herself exactly why he'd woken her this morning and her spine stiffened.

'I can guarantee that *I* won't be the cause of any unwelcome distraction in that time.'

A strange expression crossed his face before he abruptly stood up, did up his buttons and straightened his tie. When he was done, it was almost as if the brief glimpse behind the wall of royal duty hadn't happened.

Niesha wasn't sure whether to be thrilled or terrified that she'd seen the man behind the mask. And she didn't want to examine why. She watched him stride to the door, and then, unable to stop herself, she followed. 'Zufar?'

He stiffened. Then turned, one eyebrow raised.

'What are you going to do about…your brother?'

A fierce light blazed in his eyes. Then it was gone. 'He intended to disrupt my kingdom with his actions. When the time is right, he'll be dealt with appropriately.'

Meaning what? Revenge? Punishment?

'I will see you tonight.'

He left her shivering where she stood, fairly certain she wouldn't be able to withstand another bombshell.

Infidelity. Betrayal. Revenge. Was this what being an al Khalia was like? To think she'd rhapsodised about and envied them once upon a time!

She was still rubbing her hands down her chilled arms when Kadira knocked and entered.

Moments later they were back to discussing her wardrobe for her now postponed honeymoon.

And then it was time to choose from the list of tutors who would lecture her through her child psychology course.

One filled her with dread. The other with a quiet joy.

Niesha took a deep breath and vowed to cling onto the latter with everything she had.

CHAPTER SEVEN

THE ONE WEEK Zufar had accommodated to broker his sister's marriage while juggling his duties before leaving on his honeymoon turned into two.

It could've been because he received a summons from his father, which he kept postponing simply because he didn't wish to deal with Tariq. Their last meeting had ended with stiff, cold words that still rankled, and the simple truth was Zufar didn't know whether he would ever forgive his father for abdicating.

But his sister's sudden impending marriage needed explanation and whether he liked it or not his father was owed one.

Today was the day he'd made the trip to see Tariq. As he'd suspected, it hadn't been an easy one. Probably because his father hadn't once asked about state affairs or even about Zufar himself. He wore his grief like a cloak and looked even more shrunken than he'd been the last time Zufar had seen him. Or perhaps Zufar's unease was because, despite everything, a small part of him regretted cutting his father out of his wedding. He told himself he'd done it for a good reason—to keep the atmosphere stress-free and his citizens happy on his wedding day.

Out of sight out of mind, after all.

The pat statement rang hollow inside him, driving him from his desk and into a restless pacing of his office. King Tariq might have taken his absence from his son's wedding with pained stoicism but he'd taken the news of Galila's marriage to Sheikh Karim worse. The reminder that his father had once upon a time doted on Galila had further unsettled Zufar. It occurred to him that now his mother was dead, perhaps his father would want to reconnect with the children he'd disregarded for so long.

Zufar hardened his heart against the strange yearning triggered by that notion. There was no room for sentiment. His father had chosen his path, his actions forcing Zufar to choose his.

With the smooth running of the kingdom his priority, he had no space to accommodate might-have-beens.

What was done was done. And for the first time in for ever he had a moment's peace. Even Galila had finally accepted the consequences of her actions.

Zufar didn't know whether to succumb to the silly tradition of touching wood or raise a glass of cognac in honour of that rare peace. As to whether it would last was a debate he wasn't prepared to enter into right in this moment.

He arrived at the window overlooking the rose garden that had once belonged to his mother, and he clenched his teeth as the peace threatened to evaporate.

Many times, he'd toyed with having the rose bushes uprooted.

But he'd kept it as a reminder that loyalty and dedication to duty were far more valuable than the false love his mother had claimed to have for him in front of strangers, and the icy indifference she'd shown to him and his siblings behind closed doors. As for the man who'd occupied this office and this throne before him? Tariq al Khalia had been so locked in his obsession he'd failed to see his children, had forgiven his wife's infidelity, even going as far as to hide the full consequences of her actions right up until the past had crash-landed into their lives in the form of Adir and almost destroyed everything in its path. Until any hope of keeping this family together in the wake of his mother's death was gone for ever.

And then he'd fled, uncaring of the devastation he'd left behind.

Zufar's insides twisted with bitterness and a pain he wanted to will away with every ounce of his being but had found over the years was near impossible.

That too was a salutary lesson, an abiding reminder to stay away from foolish feelings and keep his trust circle to a party of one.

Those reminders had served him well, would continue to serve him well when it came to the subject of Adir. He would need to be dealt with, of course. Zufar's intelligence chief had pinpointed where Adir had gone into hiding in his desert kingdom but Zufar was in no hurry to pursue his brother. Revenge was a dish best served cold, after all.

Plus, he had a honeymoon to embark upon.

The thought of the woman who was now his Queen, his *wife*, triggered a different sensation in Zufar.

The rose bushes faded from view, his mind's eye conjuring up a vision of shy, quiet strength and surprising beauty that clenched a muscle in his belly.

At every turn his new bride surprised him. He hadn't held much in the way of expectations from the woman he'd plucked from obscurity. Even though her lack of pedigree hadn't bothered him as much as it had his councillors, he'd had reservations about her ability to rise to her position. But she'd taken on the role with an intelligence, poise and dignity that had surprised everyone, including him.

Unlike her predecessor, his mother, Niesha was not filling her diary with appointments with designers, magazine photo shoots and gossip-mongering luncheons. In fact, the occasional demand on her time for anything other than palace duties drew the small press of her lips he was beginning to recognise as signifying her displeasure.

The one thing that made her eyes light up was any activity involving children. And when it was time to take lessons from her tutor.

There were other times when he glimpsed strong emotion in her eyes, too, although after their wedding night she'd attempted to hide those emotions from him. Another earthy sensation shifted through Zufar, his manhood responding to his thought.

Those early-morning hours together were becoming an addictive means of waking her up from her nightmares. They might be sharing a bed in order to produce an heir, but that hour before sunrise was fast becoming a routine he didn't wish to abandon.

He sucked in a breath as his blood sang with fire and the pressure behind his fly thickened. His wife might have been innocent when he took her to bed, but she was swiftly gaining the status of the most memorable bed partner he'd ever had.

He frowned inwardly as the reasons for the need to awaken her each morning sliced through his mind.

Niesha claimed not to remember the subject of her nightmares, and he believed her.

Nevertheless it was a problem. One that might need addressing sooner rather than later. As was the subject of her past. All his investigators had been able to dig up so far was that she'd grown up in an orphanage on the outskirts of his capital city.

The last thing he needed was for other skeletons to fall out of his proverbial closet, but it seemed her past was a blank no one could fill.

The knock on his door in that moment was a half-blessing, freeing him from thinking about the enigma surrounding his new bride. Besides, he could do with not inviting problems where there were none, so he turned abruptly from the window.

'Enter,' he called.

Niesha entered, and he couldn't help but stare. He took in her slender form, his eyes lingering on the shadow of her cleavage, the neat little waist he'd gripped to hold her steady as he lost himself in her body, and the curve of her hips that could even now be cradling his child.

For the first time since his clinical discussions of heirs and legacies, Zufar allowed himself to wonder what their child would look like.

He frowned, pulling himself from the brink of useless daydream as she drew closer. Dressed in a burnt-orange dress that complemented her colour superbly, with her hair pulled up into some elaborate knot, she more than held her own as a queen.

And even though he'd availed himself of every inch of her body only a handful of hours ago, a gnawing hunger began to beat a restless, relentless beat through him.

She stopped before his desk, spine straight, head angled as if she'd spent a lifetime learning comportment rather than a scant two weeks, and looked him straight in the eye, sending the rush in his blood higher.

'I was told you wanted to see me?' she asked.

Zufar forced himself to focus. 'Yes.' He indicated the chair before his desk and waited for her to sit. 'I wanted to inform you that we leave for our honeymoon tomorrow. But before we do, there's one engagement today that needs to be filled.' The reason why that engagement had now fallen on Niesha made his mouth tighten. 'I need you.'

Her eyes widened a touch before they swept to the window, avoiding his gaze. He found himself wanting to capture her chin and redirect her attention to him. He blunted the need.

He couldn't afford to indulge in carnal pleasures when he had a kingdom to run.

You have a fifteen-minute window of free time, a voice whispered insidiously in his ear.

He pushed it away, striding to his desk and settling himself behind it. 'Galila's departure has left a few engagements unfulfilled. I've delegated most of them, but I need you to handle this one,' he said briskly.

'Oh, I see. How can I help?' There was a briskness to her tone that drew a frown from him despite his own effort to display the same demeanour. He liked her softer, Zufar realised.

She caught his frown, and a moment later her face was the serene mask she'd been presenting to the adoring public since she first stepped out in her role as his Queen two weeks ago. That his people had taken to her was an understatement. Everywhere she went she was met with bunches of flowers and adoring crowds. But that mask was for the public. Zufar was a little irritated that she was maintaining it when they were alone.

'Your schedule is free for the next few hours, I believe?' he enquired.

She nodded. 'Yes. It is.'

'Good. This is an opening ceremony at a local children's hospital. Galila was supposed to have attended but of course circumstances have changed.' His sister was currently in Zyria, Sheikh Karim having wasted no time in whisking her away the moment Zufar had given his agreement.

Niesha picked up the sheet he slid across the desk, scrutinising the page before setting it back down. This time when she looked at him, a genuine smile was in place. She was pleased, as he'd known she would be when the suggestion of being surrounded by children came up.

Again, he found himself wondering about his own future offspring, whether his son or daughter would be cherished by Niesha the way he'd never been by his parents. Zufar was a little taken aback to realise that hidden behind the gratification of certainty that his own child wouldn't be neglected or visited with indifference was a thread of jealousy.

Was he really jealous of his own unborn child?

'I'd be honoured to attend. I'll try not to let you down,' she said with a small smile that drifted away all too quickly.

He looked closer and saw the faint shadows beneath her eyes. 'They were expecting a princess. They're getting a queen. The honour will be theirs, I am sure of it.'

Her lips parted, as if she was going to respond, then she pressed them firmly together again.

Zufar wasn't entirely sure why his unease deepened. Rounding his desk, he drew a finger down her cheek. 'Are you well?' He noted that his tone was abrupt and felt a little irritated with himself.

She drew away under the pretext of rising to her feet. 'Of course. I had better go and get ready for this.'

He frowned as she started to walk away. 'Wait.'

'Yes?'

He strode towards her, the soft and alluring scent of her perfume tugging at him. 'I've had to add a few more appointments to the schedule on our honeymoon. It seems the lure of my Queen is too much for dignitaries to resist. I'd advise you therefore not to overtire yourself. We have a busy couple of weeks ahead of us.'

Her lashes swept down, the long silky length brushing her cheek. 'I'm glad I can be useful. It is my role here after all, isn't it?' she enquired softly with a smile that didn't quite reach her eyes and a note in her voice that further grated.

His eyes narrowed on her face but for the life of him, Zufar couldn't dig beneath her serene demeanour. The realisation that he wanted to know what was bothering her jarred him hard.

He was the King. He didn't deal in emotions.

'Yes,' he affirmed. 'It is.'

'Then I'll be ready.'

He went with her to the outer door, waved away the guard and opened the door himself. Then he stood watching her walk down the wide hallway, again struck by the dignity and grace in her stature and the smiles and reverence she commanded in her wake. He had no doubt she wouldn't let him down.

The first speech she'd given had been so in tune with his own vision that he'd wondered whether she'd conscripted his private secretary as her speechwriter. The discovery that she'd written the speech to his army veterans on her own had been a stunning surprise.

All of that though didn't explain the withdrawal he glimpsed frequently in her eyes.

Zufar returned to his desk, unable to shake off his frown or unease. For the first time in his life, he had a problem whose solution was eluding him and the reality of it jarred.

He had a wife who was shining in areas his own mother had severely lacked. At the thought of his mother, his mood plummeted. But try as he did to dismiss her from his thoughts, he found himself circling back to the woman who had given birth to him and then treated him as if he was an inconvenience.

Sure, there had been times now fading from memory when she'd bestowed a kind smile and a gentle touch. But that had been a long time ago, possibly even figments of his imagination. As he'd been prone to wondering lately, had those moments of brief affection been because she couldn't be with Adir, the child she'd truly loved?

His fingers tightened on the edge of his desk.

Was that it? Adir had spoken about the letters his mother had written to him in his youth. Letters declaring her love for him. That revelation had driven home the grating fact that all her devotion had been reserved for the child she'd never been able to claim as her own, with nothing left for her remaining children.

The unpalatable thought pierced him but it wasn't so easily dismissed on recollection of Adir's fury at their mother's funeral. Had their mother's love for her bastard son eventually faded too, usurped by the wealth and prestige she'd craved more than anything else?

Enough!

It was no use dwelling on his mother and a fruitless past he needed to move on from. Zufar planted his elbows on his desk and attempted to dig into the mountain of work awaiting his attention. But concentration was at a premium. Perhaps he should've touched wood after all, he mused bitterly.

When his private secretary knocked, Zufar tossed down his pen.

'Your Highness, your next appointment has been cancelled. The foreign minister's daughter was taken ill suddenly. I have sent flowers.'

Zufar's mouth twisted at his relief.

His foreign minister was an obsequious man, prone to rambling for an hour on an issue that required ten minutes. Reluctant to return to his sour thoughts, he rose from the desk.

'Free up my appointments for the next three hours,' he said, even before he'd fully made up his mind.

'Immediately, Your Highness. Can I arrange anything else for that time?'

'Inform my wife's motorcade not to leave without me. I'm attending the ceremony with her.'

His private secretary hid his surprise well, made a quick note on his tablet, bowed and hurried away to do his bidding.

Ten minutes later, Zufar waited in the limo as her bodyguards escorted Niesha to the car. For the sev-

eral seconds it took for her reach him, he stared, once
again arrested and a little stunned that he'd ever imagined her plain.

Sunlight glinted on her thick, luxurious hair, which
had been rearranged into another attractive knot. The
sea-green dress she'd changed into hugged her slim
torso before flaring at the waist, the skirt showing off
shapely long legs balanced on designer heels. A pulse
of satisfaction went through him as he spotted the emerald necklace he'd given to her two days ago circling
her neck.

It was part of a larger collection of jewellery that
had belonged to his grandmother, and, even though the
emerald was the smallest of the lot, it was eye-catching
on Niesha and suited her outfit perfectly.

She was truly exquisite, he observed with a curious catch in his chest and a slowly elevating heartbeat.

When his gaze rose again to trace her delicate cheekbones and wide, generous mouth, renewed hunger
punched through him.

He hurried to adjust himself or risk embarrassing
both of them as the driver held the door open for her.

She slid in and froze, her eyes widening in surprise
and then suspicion. 'What are you doing here?'

'I found myself free of obligations.'

'So you decided to come to a ribbon-cutting ceremony?'

He shrugged and reached out to secure her seat belt.
'I'm in danger of losing my position as the most popu-
lar figure in Khalia,' he mused dryly.

She didn't return his smile. 'There's no danger of
that, and even if there was, you're not vain, so there
must be another reason for your presence,' she said,

her eyes growing wary as the motorcade left the palace grounds.

'A compliment slapped away by suspicion. I don't know whether to be pleased or wounded, Niesha.'

Her face remained set in lines that suggested she wasn't too pleased by his appearance.

'What's really going on, Zufar? Do you not think I can execute my duty properly?' she asked with a trace of hurt in her voice.

'I wouldn't have given you this responsibility if I didn't think you could handle it,' he stated, a little put out by the need to explain himself.

'Then why? Don't forget I saw your itinerary in your office.'

He'd kept his schedule free to spend time with his wife. It was that simple. And that complicated, Zufar realised.

'There may be questions about Galila.'

'Questions you don't think I can handle.' It wasn't a question but a flat statement.

For a moment, he wished he'd stayed in his office after all. It was certainly an odd feeling to know his presence wasn't required. Unsettling still to acknowledge that he wasn't wanted. That brought back memories he'd dwelt on for far too long already today.

'I don't believe I owe you an explanation of how I use my time,' he added, his voice emerging a touch more tersely than he'd intended.

He caught her wince and her pinched face, and suppressed a growl.

For several minutes they travelled in silence. Then she reached into her handbag and pulled out a sheet of paper. 'Well, I'd intended to read through my speech in the car, so if you don't mind…?'

'You may practise it on me, if you wish.'

Her breath caught faintly before a wave of colour flowed into her cheeks. It took every ounce of control he could muster not to touch her in that moment. 'Are… are you sure?'

'Of course,' he replied.

She stared at him for endless moments, then gave a small nod. After straightening the sheet, she cleared her throat. And then she began to speak.

Zufar listened. Watched her. Struggled not to get lost in her husky, melodious voice. Not to get lost in the powerful message of support, the strong empathy and even the self-deprecating jokes she managed to slot in so effortlessly.

It took a few beats to realise she was done, and staring at him, eyes wide and wary.

'You wrote that by yourself in three hours?'

She immediately averted her gaze, looked down at the paper. 'Is it that bad?' Her voice was a little unsteady.

Before he could stop himself, he reached across and captured her hand. 'It's that good.'

She gasped. 'Really? Are you sure? I always worry that I'm gushing a little too hard. Or not enough.'

His thumb stroked back and forth across her hand, a strange need that had nothing to do with sex mounting higher inside him. 'There's a perfect amount of gush. But I would nix that last joke at your own expense. You can keep that one private.' *For me.*

She nodded, then began to rummage in her handbag.

He reached into the sleek compartment next to him and offered her a pen.

The smallest smile curved her lips as she took it. 'Thank you.'

A yearning to see a wider, longer-lasting smile hit him hard, but he settled for watching her amend her speech. When she was done, he took her hand again. She made no move to withdraw it, and, finding that he liked touching her silk-smooth skin far too much, he kept his hand where it was right up until they arrived at the hospital.

An excited hum of surprise went through the size-able crowd as he stepped out. Then it turned into shouts of adoration when Niesha joined him on the bright blue carpet. 'I believe my assessment is proving accurate,' he murmured.

Her smile as she waved to the crowd was warm and open. 'I'm just a passing fancy. You'll regain their total devotion before the month's out, I'm sure.'

He wasn't sure why that transitory statement rubbed him the wrong way. Perhaps it was the reminder that he'd placed a ticking-clock clause on their marriage, one that was already chiming much too loudly for his liking.

He shrugged the thought away and accompanied Niesha as she approached the crowd. As with her smile, her greeting was warm and engaging, although Zufar noticed that she gravitated towards children and moth-ers with small babies, taking time to draw a smile or laugh before she moved on.

Almost automatically, because such occasions were bred into his bones, Zufar expertly navigated the crowd until it was time to go inside.

They were given the tour, the hospital staff beside

themselves to be graced by two royals. Again Niesha lingered with the children, especially the disadvantaged ones, listening to them and reading them stories that drew smiles even from the sickest children.

When the time came for her speech, she delivered it with grace and eloquence, drawing immediate and enthusiastic applause when it was over.

But even as he experienced a satisfying swell of pride, he couldn't shake the niggling thought that, though his wife seemed to be settling into her role as his Queen, perhaps she was also counting down the time until the five years were up.

'You're frowning,' observed the deep voice.

Niesha looked up from the medical webpage she'd been reading, a little startled by Zufar's sudden appearance.

From the moment they'd taken off four hours ago, he'd been ensconced with his advisers at the front section of the stunning royal plane, leaving her with her own smaller staff. Her meeting to go over her itinerary had lasted barely an hour, after which she'd dismissed her staff and found a quieter area towards the back of the plane.

She'd needed a moment or three with her thoughts but had declined Kadira's suggestion that she head upstairs to the master bedroom to rest.

The thought of sliding into bed, with Zufar in such close proximity, sent several traitorous tingles through her body, a state she couldn't seem to block no matter how much she tried.

Besides that, there was also the fact that last night she'd noticed a little spotting when she'd taken a shower.

But this morning there'd been no trace of it. She'd debated whether to tell Zufar and decided to keep it to herself for now in case it was a false alarm.

Deep down though, Niesha knew the reason she was keeping quiet was because of the possibility that if she was pregnant, Zufar, with his duty done, might instigate separate bedrooms after all. Since that first time they'd made love, that remoteness had remained, even though he managed to skilfully draw sensations from her she'd never thought possible. He was an undeniable expert in the bedroom, and a huge part of her was terrified that she'd already grown addicted to her husband's touch.

Very quickly their time in bed, especially in the dawn hours when he drew her from a restless sleep, had become the highlight of her day. And try as she might she couldn't find the strength to give it up just yet.

So she closed her tablet and the page that gave dire predictions for spotting during pregnancy, uncrossed her legs and attempted to school her features. Thankfully, when she raised her gaze, his was on her legs. A moment later, probing eyes met hers, and his eyebrow quirked as he awaited a response.

She grimaced. 'I unwittingly clicked on a link while I was reviewing a list of charities. I told you not everyone was enamoured of me.'

It was a smaller, safer truth in a greater list of things on her mind.

He sank onto his haunches, surprising her a little, and then set her heartbeat soaring by bringing his masculine perfection even closer. His clean, musky aftershave drifted over her, sending vivid images of how shamelessly she lost herself in it when they made love.

'Do yourself a favour and ignore them,' he dismissed offhandedly. 'You don't need the headache, and I don't want an overwrought wife on our honeymoon.'

'I like to think I'm made of sterner stuff than that.'

'Then why do you have shadows beneath your eyes?'

She stiffened. 'Is that your way of telling me I look a mess?'

'It's my way of saying you should've taken your secretary's advice and gone upstairs to bed.'

She wasn't even going to ask how he knew that. 'Are you here to order me to bed?' she retorted, cringingly noting the huskiness in her voice.

His eyes blazed for a moment before they cleared. Rising gracefully to his feet, he held out his hand. 'That is precisely what I'm doing. We don't land for another three hours. I'll make sure you're woken before then.'

Disappointment followed hard on the heels of the breathlessness that seized her. She was so busy trying to hide it she let herself be pulled up and tugged up the stairs.

The bedroom took up the whole smaller top deck of the plane, and was so dreamily, jaw-droppingly beautiful, Niesha would've been completely lost in it had Zufar's riveting presence beside her not commanded her attention.

She barely heard the door snick shut behind her, but she was intensely aware of his overwhelming presence, the dizzyingly broad width of his shoulders as he drew her towards the bed. Her heart began thundering as he plucked the tablet from her hand and deftly tossed back the coverlet on the king-sized bed.

The jacket of the stylish navy trouser suit she'd worn for the flight came off neatly under his ministrations, leaving a cream silk camisole that suddenly felt too hot against her skin. Her nipples were beginning to pebble and that dragging sensation had started low in her belly.

Niesha shook her head when his hands went to her hair, intent on removing the diamond clip holding it up. 'I really don't need help undressing. Nor do I need to rest at all. I'm f—'

'You're not fine,' he interrupted. 'You spent the night tossing and turning.' The grim set to his face told her he wasn't pleased. 'Another nightmare?'

It was easier to nod to that than admit that her suspicion of her new condition was what had disturbed her sleep. 'I'm sorry if I bothered you.'

He dismissed her apology with a wave of his hand, and stepped forwards with renewed intention of freeing her hair. This time he succeeded. 'How long have you had them?'

She steeled herself against the clutch of pain confessing the truth brought. 'For as long as I can remember. I think the only thing that will stop them is a full account of the years I lost before I ended up in the orphanage.' She wasn't sure why she let that slip but once it was out there, she couldn't take it back.

He stilled. 'Perhaps you should consider reconciling yourself to the possibility that you might never know,' he suggested after a moment.

Hurt lanced through her. Her heart thundered louder as she took in his grim expression. Would this flaw in her lineage reap consequences down the line? Make her a damaged queen? 'You think I haven't tried? That I want my subconscious to keep dredging it up every night?'

His eyes narrowed. 'Calm yourself—'

Hurt built up higher. 'That's easy for you to say, isn't it? You've had your whole life documented a few hundred different ways from the moment you drew breath. All you need to do is pluck a book off a shelf and you can refresh your memory on even the tiniest detail. Well, I'm glad you can be so glib about me forgetting my past but you'll excuse me if I don't feel the same!'

'Enough, Niesha. I won't have you distressing yourself,' he commanded with a bite to his deep, masterful voice.

But she wasn't in the mood to heed this warning. 'And I won't have you ordering me about, telling me when to go to bed or telling me how to feel!'

Perhaps it was the reality that she might be pregnant that sent her emotions into free fall. Or the dire predictions for her spotting she'd foolishly looked up on the Internet. She'd done it as a means of alleviating her worry but had ended up even more distressed.

Because thinking about the child she would possibly be having nine months from now, she'd been confronted with the fact that one day her son or daughter would ask about her past. And she wouldn't have an answer for them. One side of their family tree would be full to brimming with generations of history, and the other side, *hers*, would be woefully empty.

Zufar started to raise his hand.

She shook her head wildly, knocking his hand away. 'I don't want your sympathy. Or your directives. I want… I want you to leave me alone!'

He completely disregarded her request, strong hands gripping her shoulders to pull her into his hard, brick-wall body.

One hand was splayed on her back while the other

captured her nape, trapping her against his impressive length. Before she could protest, both hands began a languorous kneading, digging with gentle pressure into muscles knotted tight with tension.

She parted her lips on a gasp that never made it because he was kissing her, his tongue delving between her lips to boldly stroke her tongue.

The resulting effect of the outer caress and the inner melting was so wonderfully divine, she moaned helplessly. Then kept moaning as he deepened both caresses, rending her mindless as her knees weakened and she sagged against him.

The floating effect continued even after he'd laid her on the bed and levered himself over her without breaking the kiss. His thighs bracketed hers as he continued to hold her tight against his body, ravaging her lips, flooding her whole being and especially her sex with warmth and desire and so, so much hunger.

This.

This was the addiction she already feared she would never be free of.

With a strangled cry, she spiked her fingers into his hair and threw herself into the kiss, her body writhing against his.

She was fairly sure he didn't remain as removed or as silent this time. Or perhaps the muted growl she heard might have been the hum of jet engines.

Niesha didn't really care.

All she wanted, all she *craved* was for him to keep wrecking her with his potent kiss, his magic hands. He cupped her breast, moulded her flesh before mercilessly teasing its tight peak.

'Zufar...' She gasped.

The plane hit a pocket of deep turbulence, rudely jarring them apart.

For an eternity Zufar stared down at her, his breathing harsh, his face a tight mask of unbridled hunger. Hunger he mastered before her stunned eyes seconds before launching himself off her to stride several steps away.

'Zufar…'

He rounded on her, his face under even tighter control. 'My apologies,' he bit out thickly. 'I didn't mean for things to get so carried away. It won't happen again.'

She wasn't sure whether the chill that descended on her was because he was apologising for touching her or for the hint of self-loathing she caught in his voice. Both, she suspected.

The reality that their lovemaking was really only about duty for Zufar lanced like forked lightning through her. Every anguished cell in her body wanted to curl up in a ball. But she forced herself to remain contained, to rise and force her weak legs towards the door she hoped led to the bathroom. 'No need to apologise. You were looking for a way to calm your hysterical wife. Don't worry,' she threw over her shoulder, 'I'll be the picture of composure by the time we land.'

With that she thrust the door open, glimpsed the porcelain sink and shower stall, and rushed inside, locking the door behind her.

She avoided her gaze in mirror as she splashed water over her wrists and face. Then, knowing she couldn't go out and face him, not just yet, she braced her back against the door, wrapping her arms around her middle as she fought the tears that were determined to fall.

Niesha wasn't sure how long she spent in the bathroom, but by the time she emerged he was gone. Yet relief was nowhere in sight. Not when the dawning suspicion that, far from being a thing of the past, her childhood crush on Zufar seemed to have resurfaced, and, much stronger this time, now loomed like a spectre on her horizon.

CHAPTER EIGHT

TRUE TO HIS WORD, the incident on the plane didn't happen again. Nor did Zufar make any attempt to touch her either during the night or in the early hours of the morning as he'd previously done.

By the sixth day of their honeymoon tour, Niesha was beginning to think she was one of the unfortunate few women who wouldn't experience the most intimate part of her honeymoon. And while a greater part of her desperately struggled with the loss of his touch, a tiny, self-preserving part of her urged her to count her blessings.

She hadn't been able to completely expel the niggling voice that whispered she was much more invested emotionally than she was willing to admit. Because it couldn't be true. Not so soon. Not so foolishly.

So she pushed the voice away, joined Zufar for breakfast each morning before they made whatever appearance in whatever museum or charity or luncheon they were supposed to attend, where she gazed adoringly at him, waved at the crowd and pinned the smile on her face until the photographers had their money shots.

After that he had her driven back to whatever splendid hotel or villa or mansion they were staying at while he went off to conduct business, and she was supposed to spend endless hours getting ready for another evening function.

Tonight, it was a ball being thrown in their honour by the Khalian Ambassador to Italy. They'd arrived in Venice last night and visited all the main sights this morning. After Dubai, Prague and London, the magnificent sights were beginning to blur into one. But Venice had been truly breathtaking, something she wasn't going to forget in a hurry.

But as she dressed in a sweeping, strapless dove-grey silk gown, overlaid with soft chiffon mesh, into which delicate butterflies had been sewn, Niesha's heartbeat began to thud faster.

Her period still hadn't arrived.

And she really couldn't hold back from telling Zufar any longer. For all she knew, he had the exact dates of her monthly cycle memorised. Was that another reason for his sudden lack of interest?

She tried to breathe through the heavy, unbearable weight that pressed on her chest as Halimah settled the small diamond tiara on her head. Apparently it was customary headwear for all overseas Khalian-hosted functions.

After the second day, she'd given up keeping track of protocol when it came to her attire and jewels and let Halimah take over.

Like now, she tuned out a little as she was primped and made up. But her smile of thanks was genuine, as were the butterflies fluttering wildly in her stomach as she left the suite and headed to the living room.

Zufar stood at the glass window of their villa, his gaze hovering in the middle distance as he nursed a cognac. For a moment she was struck genuinely dumb at the magnificent figure he cut in his tuxedo.

Truly, no man had the right to look this good, this powerful, this rawly masculine. And yet the evidence was right there before her eyes. Irrefutable. Dangerous to her senses.

She inhaled shakily and audibly, enough to drag him from wherever he was. He swivelled to face her, and Niesha wanted to groan with the indecency of his breathtaking face.

She swallowed the sound, curled her fingers around her minuscule clutch to keep from doing something foolish like reaching out for him as he approached.

He didn't speak. Not immediately. Instead, his gaze rested for a long time on the tiara, then conducted a lazy inspection of her from head to toe. 'You look exceptionally beautiful,' he breathed.

The faintest hint of cognac and mint wafted over her face and she wanted to close her eyes, taste him from the source. Instead she locked her knees. 'You don't look so bad yourself.'

Her words sounded stilted, even to her own ears. He didn't react, merely inclined his head before handing off his glass to a hovering attendant and holding out his arm. 'Shall we?'

The sleek speedboat they boarded took them smoothly down the Grand Canal and beneath the Rialto Bridge before traversing a series of smaller canals. Their destination was another architectural masterpiece that took her breath away.

The Chiesa Palace was owned by Zufar but loaned to the embassy for its residence. She knew from absorbing royal history that it had been painstakingly restored from a crumbling heap to its former glory, including the stunning cathedral windows, the priceless paintings that had almost perished during wars and floods, and the chandeliers made of crystal and Murano glass.

Everything in sight glittered and gleamed as they stepped onto the red carpet and greeted the long line of guests awaiting their arrival.

Halfway down the line, her heel caught in the carpet and Niesha stumbled. Zufar immediately caught her, righting her with a sharp look.

'Are you all right?' he murmured, ignoring the guest in front of them waiting to be greeted.

'Yes, I'm fine,' she said, somehow managing to keep the smile pinned on her face.

A moment later, Zufar's hand settled on her back. The branding heat of his hand and the act itself was so unsettling, warmth flushed through her.

She wanted to lean into him, absorb even more of him. Which resulted in holding herself stiffly until they were in the stunning reception room of the palazzo.

'You…you can let go of me now.'

Tawny eyes scoured her face, as if he was searching for something. A moment later, his hand dropped.

Immediately she wanted his touch back. Cursing her traitorous body, she slid into diplomatic mode, smiling and conversing, and even managing to waltz with Zufar without letting her emotions slip.

But it was a drain on her senses. So the moment they returned to their villa, and had a moment of privacy, she gathered her courage and faced him. 'Zufar, we need to talk.'

His face tightened, and he stiffened as if bracing himself for a blow. 'To my knowledge those words either herald catastrophe or something…different. I've yet to experience the latter but do go on,' he rasped.

'It's up to you how you view the news that I think I'm pregnant.'

As Niesha was beginning to recognise, the wheels of royalty and privilege were programmed to turn so smoothly and efficiently, she barely noticed their motion.

Since becoming Queen, in her every waking moment, she only had to lift a finger for her tiniest request to be put into action. And sometimes even that wasn't necessary, a seemingly telepathic connection of the staff accurately deciphering her desires before she knew about them herself.

So she shouldn't have been surprised when a team of physicians trailed into their living room suite moments after their arrival in Paris the next day.

She was sure that had it not been after midnight when she'd voiced the possibility that she might be pregnant, he would have summoned them to the palazzo in Venice.

The sensation that her world was spinning out of control wouldn't abate. Heart racing, she pulled the lapels of her elegant silk lounging wrap more firmly around her as a suited Zufar approached where she stood on the terrace, trying in vain to distract herself with the view of the Eiffel Tower.

'The doctors are here,' he said.

'Do we need to do this now?' she hedged, unable to stop the scenarios that reeled through her head, all ending with the unassailable fact that if she was confirmed pregnant, her honeymoon would be over.

True, her supposed honeymoon had been filled

with accompanying Zufar to endless engagements and smiling through luncheons and state dinners when she would rather be curled up with a book in one of the quieter rooms of their royal suite.

But during those events, she had a front-row seat to the daily life and work of the man she'd married. No longer did she have to watch him on a TV screen or gaze at glossy, still pictures in a magazine.

She'd watched in real life as he'd negotiated a trade deal over pre-dinner cocktails with little more than a handful of sentences. She'd listened, stunned, as he'd given his frank opinion on a decades-long border dispute between bitter enemies, only to see it implemented days later. Last night she'd looked on, her heart melting, as he'd charmed the eight-year-old daughter of his ambassador.

Who cared that he barely said more than a handful of words to her throughout their engagements? Fine, she cared. No one liked being ignored.

But still, those times she spent with him, secretly hoping she would absorb even a little of his effortless ability to govern and charm? Niesha…liked it, she admitted reluctantly. Watching him navigate the sometimes choppy waters of diplomacy was a sight she wasn't ready to be rid of despite the dangerous waters her heart waded into.

She didn't need to be a genius to know that the moment her pregnancy was confirmed she would be whisked back to Khalia. If he wasn't touching her on their honeymoon she could guarantee they would resort to separate beds, like his parents, on their return. On the other hand, if her pregnancy wasn't confirmed then…

The idea that she was hoping she wasn't pregnant

just for a chance to stay in Zufar's bed for a little longer struck her in equal parts with shame—for being so weak—and with a hunger she couldn't dismiss.

'It needs to be done, according to royal protocol,' he pronounced, in answer to her question. There was no gentleness to his tone, only a firm recital of purpose and duty. 'I'm assured it won't take long.' At her continued hesitation, he beckoned with a commanding hand. 'Come.'

Little one.

He hadn't used the endearment since their wedding night and even as she mocked herself for the absurdity of missing it, she couldn't deny that its absence left a small hollow inside her.

Firmly, she pushed that sensation away, then forced herself not to dwell on the fact that his hand dropped to his side when she approached him, instead of reaching for hers as he did when they were out in public.

Those moments were for show, she reminded herself. Zufar and Niesha al Khalia had been hailed as the world's most photogenic and romantic royal couple. She barely managed to stop her lips from twisting.

If only they knew.

So, as she'd trained herself to do, she went to his side, making sure to keep a small distance between them as they re-entered the living room.

There were three physicians in total, two male and one female, all of middle age, and a younger male intern who bowed as they approached.

'I'm Dr Wadya. We will not keep you very long, Your Highness,' the female doctor promised with a smile.

A little more at ease, Niesha acknowledged other introductions and took a seat on the sofa. Zufar took his place behind her, one hand resting lightly on the seat a hair's breadth from her shoulder. When she was instructed to, she removed her wrap, handed it to an attendant hovering nearby, then resisted the urge to run her sweaty palms down the thighs of her silk slip dress.

Try as she might, she couldn't stop her racing heart. Not when she, and everyone in the room, were holding their collective breaths at the possibility that she could be carrying Zufar's heir.

The drumming in her ears precluded her from hearing what was being discussed. In a way it was a blessing because she could temporarily forget that her life was being planned and plotted around her.

Still, she heard the sharp inhalation from the older male doctor, Dr Basim.

'What is it?' Zufar enquired sharply.

The man's pale-faced gaze was fixed on the birthmark on her forearm. He gave a slight shake of his head, but remained silent, his focus on the pink starfish mark that resided on the inside of her arm just below her inner elbow.

She frowned, her heart lurching as she looked at the faces of the doctors.

'Is something wrong?' she asked.

As if dragged from a stupor, Dr Basim's rose gaze from her arm. 'I'm sure it's just a coincidence,' he said.

'What is a coincidence?' Zufar bit out. 'Explain yourself, if you please.' The statement was less request, more directive.

'I don't wish to jump to conclusions, Your Highness,' the doctor said. 'I merely thought I recognised the mark on Her Highness's arm.'

Tense silence descended on the room. Niesha's breath

strangled in her throat as everyone remained frozen in place.

Zufar moved, his elegant hand flicking in a subtle command that got everyone moving. The young intern approached with the equipment and swiftly set it up.

Niesha barely acknowledged the process, her heart racing now for a completely different reason. The moment they were done, Zufar dismissed everyone save for Dr Basim.

'How do you recognise it?' she blurted, unable to keep the question inside.

Dr Basim shook his head. 'It's nothing. I don't wish to alarm you, Your Highness. My apologies.'

She wanted to protest that it wasn't nothing, not when his reaction had been so strong. But one look at Zufar's closed expression and she held her tongue. Numbly, she watched Dr Basim prepare to leave.

She wasn't sure why she jumped up and trailed him as he left the living room. But as they approached the door, she knew she couldn't let it go. Something was wrong. 'So, what now?' she asked, watching the doctor.

Dr Basim paused and turned around. 'Your Highness?'

'How long before we know whether my wife is pregnant or not?' Zufar slid in.

It wasn't what she had meant to ask, but she held her breath all the same. 'The blood tests will reveal if there's a pregnancy within a matter of hours, Your Highness.'

Zufar nodded.

She watched the doctor reach for the doorknob. 'Wait.'

Beside her Zufar stiffened. 'Niesha? What is it?' he

enquired softly, even though the set of his jaw showed that he was as puzzled by her reaction as she was herself.

'I have some questions,' she addressed Dr Basim. 'Can you please stay for a few more minutes?'

As the royal doctor, he couldn't very well refuse, and she was selfishly counting on that.

Acutely aware that Zufar followed closely behind, she returned to the living room. Then before she could lose her courage, she faced the two men. 'What do you know about me?' she asked Dr Basim boldly.

The doctor's eyes widened, and he slid a quick glance at Zufar. But Zufar's narrow-eyed glance was on her face. It remained there for a long time before he turned to the doctor. 'Answer my wife's question.'

Dr Basim hesitated. 'Your Highness…'

Niesha shook her head. 'You have my word that you won't be in any trouble. I only wish to know what you thought when you saw the mark on my arm. You recognised something about it. Am I right?'

Zufar tensed even harder, then he redirected his gaze to the doctor. 'Did you?' he demanded.

Dr Basim's unease grew.

'Please… I need to know.'

She stared down at the starfish mark on her arm, which had started to throb and burn as if yearning for its secret to be set free. Something inside her told her to push the doctor. Something unstoppable.

Zufar turned to the older man. 'Is she right? Do you know something?'

Dr Basim took a deep steadying breath and then slowly nodded. 'Perhaps I do.'

She lunged forwards before she could stop myself. 'What?'

'Before I emigrated to Khalia, I was a citizen of Rumadah.' He named the small country nestled in the most southerly point between the Middle East and Africa, known to many as a desert paradise, rich in oil. The only other facts she knew about the small kingdom were those she'd read in glossy magazines.

'Go on,' she urged with a voice that croaked a little.

'I had the honour of being the royal physician, right up until…' He paused, a wave of anguish unfurling over his face.

'Yes?' Zufar prodded impatiently.

Dr Basim cleared his throat. 'The royal family were on a private family holiday when tragedy struck.'

Zufar stilled, his whole body assuming the appearance of a granite statue. His eyes darted to Niesha before returning to the doctor. 'You were the royal family's personal doctor?' he pressed.

'What were their names? What happened to them?' she cried, unable to keep her emotions bottled.

Eyes reflecting pain met hers. 'As far as I am aware, Your Highness, a tyre exploded and their vehicle veered off a bridge while they were visiting a resort in Zyria. It burst into flames on impact and the whole family perished.'

She staggered backwards, swaying on her feet. The next moment Zufar was in front of her, taking her by the elbows and placing her in the seat. 'Stay there,' he instructed firmly under his breath.

Turning around, he faced the doctor again. 'I vaguely recall the incident but what has it got to do with my wife?'

The older man's gaze dropped to where she was still absently rubbing at the birthmark. 'The King's five-

year-old daughter had the exact same birthmark as Her
Highness. It was what made me think that there could
be a connection...' He stopped, realising the enormity
of his words. 'Or it could just be a coincidence.'

'You don't think so, otherwise you wouldn't have
reacted so strongly,' Zufar countered.

Dr Basim spread his hands in apology.

The rock that lodged itself in Niesha's chest threatened to choke her, cutting off the air to her lungs and
any possibility that she'd, *at last*, found some answers.

The hope she'd wildly entertained turned to ash in
her mouth.

She dropped her head and fought the tears that stung
her eyes. Words had lost meaning the moment he'd mentioned the bridge. The accident he spoke of had happened in Zyria. According to the matrons, she'd been
found wandering in a ravine in Khalia.

Nowhere near a bridge or a resort.

Besides, the thought that she could be associated
with royalty was absurd. Because surely if that was the
case, other members of her family or *someone* would've
come looking for her?

'When exactly did the accident happen?' Zufar probed.

Dr Basim's gaze grew thoughtful. 'Twenty years
ago.'

Her heart lurched again, but she shook her head.
It wasn't her. It couldn't be. The truth was, she would
never know her real family. She needed to accept it, especially now that she was possibly pregnant with her
own child. She needed to look ahead, forge a future for
her children without clinging to the past.

She summoned a smile at Dr Basim. 'Thank you for
your time. That's all I wanted to know.'

She caught Zufar's frown, but he dismissed the doctor with a casual wave of his hand. She remained frozen in the seat as they walked away. Once again her hopes had been dashed. She would never really know who she was, where she came from or if she belonged to anyone.

Even now, despite her title and the ring on her finger, she didn't belong. She was just a vessel to carry al Khalia heirs.

It should be enough.

It is enough, she affirmed to herself. But the reassurance rang hollow, the pain in her heart not letting it take root. The anguish of knowing she would never find answers wrapped itself around her heart, squeezing every last bit of her hope out of her.

She attempted to straighten her face as Zufar returned, and swallowed when he placed himself directly in front of her. The look in his eyes was intently speculative, drawing a small shiver across her skin. 'What?' she asked.

'You may be carrying my child. The need to discover your past burns strongly but it would please me greatly if you didn't distress yourself unduly over it.'

A laugh scraped its way out of her throat. 'You heard what the doctor said. These…people perished in Zyria. I was found in Khalia. There's no connection.'

His eyes darkened a touch and his mouth pulled in a firm line. His whole body thrummed with tension. 'Nevertheless you are disappointed. And emotional. I may not have experienced what you're going through but that doesn't mean I don't empathise.'

Her eyes began to prickle all over again. 'Thank you.'

He nodded. 'And while you may not believe there's

a connection, I will instruct my investigators to dig a little deeper with the new information we have. When Dr Basim returns, he'll provide the additional information we need.'

She inhaled sharply, astonishment bursting through her. 'You want to help me?'

'Why does that surprise you when my investigators already attempted once?'

Her shrug didn't quite hit the mark. 'I don't know,' she floundered, 'maybe because you said you preferred me to be a blank slate?'

His face closed, and then he nodded. 'I don't want any surprises, but I also don't want you to distress yourself over the question of your past.' His eyes dropped to where she was rubbing her birthmark. 'It's a matter that needs to be resolved one way or the other. I wish it to be sooner.'

Because of the baby.

Her heart thudded dully inside her. Everything needed to be smooth so nothing disturbed any pregnancy, now or in the future. She wasn't sure why the offer bruised her. She should be glad he was putting his considerable resources and authority behind the quest to find her past.

Still she shook her head. 'There's nothing to find,' she said flatly, unable to rouse any enthusiasm for the task. 'I asked the matrons at the orphanage for years and they had no clue what happened to me before I was found near that ravine. I was miles away from civilisation and no one came forwards then or afterwards. It's a waste of time.'

His lips compressed. 'With respect, I have a little more clout than your matrons.'

She nodded. 'I know, but I still don't want you to waste your time.'

'Because you are afraid of further disappointment?'

A burst of anger propelled her to her feet. 'What's that supposed to mean?'

'Calm yourself, Niesha,' he warned silkily.

'You're doing it again,' she snapped.

His eyes narrowed. 'And you're getting agitated. It's not good for your condition.'

She laughed. 'What condition? We haven't even verified that I'm pregnant yet,' she exclaimed wildly.

'But you know. Don't you, Niesha?' His voice was like the softest, most potent magic, weaving its way through her as he caught her by the shoulders. 'You know you're carrying my child.'

Helplessly, she swayed against him. 'Our child. It's *ours*.' She had no past to claim, but this…*this* she would claim.

He captured her chin, propelled her gaze to his. The stark possessiveness that gleamed in his eyes stopped her breath. A heartbeat later, his hand dropped to splay over her flat belly, and his chest expanded in a long inhalation. 'Indeed, it is ours. And we will *both* make its well-being our priority.'

There was something so final in those words that she shifted on her feet.

'Enough fretting,' he commanded thickly without raising his voice. 'Stay.'

Perhaps it was the electrifying effect of this touch, or the deep timbre of his voice. But she stilled, unable to look away from the gold depths as he gazed down at her.

His eyes raked her face a moment before he swung her up in his arms. With quick, sure strides he went down the wide hallway into the master suite. She thought he would leave her there, and her pulse rocketed wildly as he drew back the sheets and joined her in bed.

But all Zufar did was press a kiss to her forehead before drawing her into his arms. 'I've cancelled our appointments for the day. You will rest until Dr Basim returns.'

A part of her wanted to protest at his high-handedness. But really what was the use? He was the King. And she…she was cocooned in warm, powerful arms, her thoughts already beginning to drift away, as if reacting to his directive. With a sigh, she snuck her arm around his waist, rested her head on his shoulder and let her senses succumb to nothingness.

She would need her strength for when Dr Basim returned with further disappointment and heartache. Until then…

She was pregnant. Of course she was.

Zufar's seed had most likely taken root on their wedding night. Her heart sang wildly with a mixture of joy and apprehension as she listened to the doctors' instructions on how to take care of the royal baby in her womb.

She glanced at Zufar as the doctors rattled on about vitamins and healthy eating. Besides the initial gleam that lit his eyes, his face was an inscrutable mask. As for her, she couldn't stop her gaze from darting to the briefcase Dr Basim had brought with him.

It stood beside his chair, offering dangerous hope she couldn't stem.

A noise echoed through the room. When Zufar's eyes narrowed on her, she realised it'd come from her.

'That will be all,' he said abruptly. 'Thank you. Dr Basim, you will remain.'

The others bowed and filed out. Sensing suspense wouldn't be tolerated, the doctor reached for his brief-case. 'Your Highness, I've consulted my old notes. We'll need to do further tests, of course, but the blood type I have on file matches yours. And I've gathered pictures of all royal skin markings including the Princess and your…um… King Nazir's. The one of the Princess is an identical match to yours.'

King Nazir. Her father. Maybe.

A jagged whimper left her throat. Zufar's warm hand enfolded hers, lending her much-needed strength. 'What…what was his…their full names?'

Zufar answered, 'Your father's name is…was…King Nazir Al-Bakar, Sheikh of Rumadah, and your mother was Queen Ayeesha. If the records are correct you also had an older brother, Jamil, who perished in the crash. Your own name is Princess Nazira Fatima Al-Bakar, named after your father.'

Nazira not Niesha.

She had a name. A history. But she was still all alone.

Her cracked heart broke into further pieces at the thought of the parents and brother she would never meet, never share a smile or a joke with. Never con-fess her worries to or share theirs. 'How did you know?' she croaked.

'I did some research of my own while you were asleep.'

'A-and?' Her voice shook horribly but she was past caring.

'And you are the exact likeness of your mother,' Zufar delivered with a deep, low voice. 'In hindsight, it's astonishing how the similarities could've been missed.'

Shock continued to reel through her. In some distant corner of her mind, she knew she was crying but she couldn't help her tears. 'Because no one was looking for a pr-princess in an orphanage. Or in a chambermaid's uniform.'

Silence throbbed as her words seeped into their very bones. A moment later, Zufar handed her a handkerchief.

She dabbed her eyes, then refocused on the doctor. 'You said you'll need to do further tests?'

'Your blood type is rare. So was your father's. Because of that we kept samples in storage in case they were needed for surgery. Comparing yours to his won't be a problem.'

'But how can they still be in storage twenty years later?'

'The laws of your kingdom prohibit the destruction or disposal of a king's property for twenty-five years in case of his sudden death and no heir apparent. But besides the blood, there are other forms of DNA we can test. With your permission, of course, Your Highness.'

Niesha nodded numbly, shock holding her prisoner. 'I… Of course. You have my permission.' She bit her lip, unable to contain what was happening to her. 'But… how is it that I ended up in Khalia and not Zyria with my family?'

Zufar's hand tightened on hers. 'The place where the tragedy happened was very close to the border with Khalia, separated by a deep ravine. I think you were thrown clear when the accident happened and you wandered off.'

'What? But I was only five years old.'

'I only met you a few times, Your Highness, but you struck me as very determined, even at such a young age. You may have gone to seek help and got lost. Or you may just have been disorientated, the trauma wiped from your memory by the time you were discovered,' Dr Basim said.

Niesha realised then that she would never truly have all the answers she sought. But there was one deep, burning curiosity she could satisfy. She licked her dry lips and nodded to the sleek tablet lying on the coffee table. 'Can I see… Do you have pictures of my family?'

'Of course,' Zufar said, reaching for the tablet.

Seconds later, she found herself staring into eyes that looked so much like her own, further tears welled. Her mother was delicately beautiful, like a rare flower. Her father stood tall, broad-shouldered in traditional clothes. His eyes were darker than hers but, within the depths, Niesha recognised herself. Her soul.

She moved to another picture. In this one, a candid shot probably taken in between more scripted ones, her parents were staring at each other with such utter devotion that the camera was an intrusion. Her gaze moved to her brother and her heart began to break all over again.

Jamil.

Eight at the time of his death, he bore all the hallmarks of turning out just like their father.

Lastly, she located a picture of herself as a child. She wore a deep lavender dress with a white ribbon tied at the waist. The ribbons were replicated in her hair and she was beaming at the camera, leaning forwards with the eagerness and impatience of a five-year-old. Her hands were propped on her knees, and there, clear as day, was the starfish imprinted on her skin.

At the sight of the birthmark, another sob escaped.

'Niesha.' Zufar's voice held a throb of concern, but she waved him away.

'I'm fine, I promise.'

She scrolled through until she found a video interview of her parents. They were about to celebrate some event and had given a few minutes to a reporter. Fingers shaking, Niesha hit the play button. Her father was speaking, his deep, baritone voice authoritative but warm.

And then her mother spoke.

Niesha gasped, a deep trembling seizing her body as she listened to her mother's voice. The voice she carried in her head. The voice that soothed her in times of distress…was her mother's voice.

'Mother…'

She didn't feel the tablet slipping from her fingers.

Or the tight curse from Zufar before he caught her in his arms.

All she felt was blessed darkness.

CHAPTER NINE

SHE WOKE UP propped against soft pillows, the thick coverlet pulled up to her chest.

'What happened?'

Zufar's mouth tightened and his darkened eyes scoured her face. 'You fainted after hearing your mother's voice.'

Memories rushed back, buffeting her with profound sadness. But beside that emotion there was a curious warmth, a lessening of the hollowness that had been part of her life for so long.

Her mother's voice.

It had stayed with her all these years, assuring her that she wasn't truly alone. That she was loved.

Tears began to well again, but she blinked them back, if for no other reason than because she was sure any more tears would make Zufar confine her to bed indefinitely. She couldn't allow that, not when there was so much more to learn about her family. About herself.

Absently, she noticed her wrist being tugged and turned her head to see Dr Basim taking her pulse. She held her breath as he finished up.

'Well?' Zufar demanded.

'She's fine, Your Highness.' Dr Basim smiled at her.

'As long as you take it easy, the episode shouldn't happen again.'

'It shouldn't have happened at all,' Zufar stated with a near growl.

'I'm fine. Really.'

'So you keep telling me. And yet the evidence tells a different story.'

Dr Basim tucked his stethoscope away. 'I'll leave you to rest.'

'Wait,' Niesha rose off the bed, only to be firmly tucked back in by Zufar. Her glare merely bounced off him. She redirected her gaze to Dr Basim.

'Can we… Can we keep this confidential? I don't want anything to get out until…in case it's a false alarm.'

The doctor smiled. 'I'm almost certain it won't be, Your Highness—'

'Nevertheless, I want your word that nothing about this will get out until we have an answer one way or the other. Zufar… I mean, Khalia can do without the upheaval right now.'

Beside her, she saw her husband's imperceptible stiffening. 'You're thinking about me? My people? In this moment?' There was a trace of astonishment in his voice.

'They're my people too, aren't they? They deserve better than to have another bombshell thrown in their laps.'

An emotion shifted across his face, gone before she could read it properly. 'You forget that our marriage ended up being less of a bombshell and more of a welcome celebration.'

'And I'd like to keep it that way for as long as I can, if you don't mind,' she said.

Again something gleamed in his eyes, arresting her focus, not that she needed much to take her focus from Zufar's face. Everything he did, every breath he took seemed to captivate her in some way.

In all ways.

She wasn't sure how long they stared at each other.

A discreet cough reminded her the doctor was still in the room.

Zufar was the first to regain himself by standing and sliding his hands into his pockets. 'You will do as my wife says. Keep the circle of trust small and tight. Report directly to us once you've done your tests.'

The doctor executed an elegant bow. 'Of course. It will be exactly as you wish.'

'A private jet will be chartered to fly you to Rumadah today. We're returning to Khalia tonight. You have forty-eight hours to present us with your findings there.'

The doctor bowed again and left. Zufar crossed the suite to the phone and picked it up.

Unable to lie still, Niesha rose and padded to the window. Through the window of their presidential suite in the heart of Paris, the Seine glistened sinuously in the sunshine and the spear of the Eiffel Tower looked almost close enough to touch.

But this time the view didn't hold as much appeal. Alternate waves of heat and cold surged through her as she wrapped her hands around herself.

'I suspect I'll have a fight on my hands if I suggest you return to bed but I have ordered an early lunch for you and you will eat something.'

She rounded on him, her heart pounding. 'What if

I'm not this…this person? What if all of this is a wild coincidence?'

'It's not,' he replied. 'The pictures alone prove your connection. Besides, you were the only one unaccounted for following the accident. You were most likely presumed dead because no one expected a five-year-old to survive such an incident.'

Another shiver danced down her spine. A moment later, warm hands cupped her shoulders, then drew down her arms.

'You are the Princess. It's time you start believing it,' Zufar commanded, his deep voice sending a different sort of shiver through her.

The small laugh she gave held a touch of hysteria. 'I don't know that I can. It all feels so…overwhelming. And so messy for you.' She gave a pained laugh. 'Perhaps you would've been better off going after Amira, after all.'

His hands tightened fractionally. 'I've found that it's useless dwelling on things we cannot change.'

Her insides shrank a little that he didn't issue a firm denial of any desire for his ex-fiancée. Because deep down it was what she'd been selfishly, hungrily angling for.

'As for things being overwhelming, you proved that you can handle overwhelming when you married me three weeks ago.' That odd note she'd heard a little while ago pulsed through his voice, but, scrutinising his face, Niesha couldn't decipher his thoughts.

'If my name really isn't Niesha, do I have to change it?'

'I expect you can do whatever you please. You are

the Queen of Khalia. And soon to be confirmed as the rightful heiress to the throne of Rumadah.'

She gasped. 'But...how will that work?'

For a single moment, his jaw clenched tight, and Niesha was reminded that whatever happened to her would also cause Zufar, and more importantly Khalia, huge upheaval.

The very thing he'd striven to avoid by marrying her.

'With very careful strategising,' was all he said before he released her.

Before she could speak, a member of his staff wheeled a trolley onto the grand terrace, where a table had been set for two.

Despite her inner turmoil, Niesha forced herself to finish the vichyssoise starter. She was eating for two, after all.

She saw the gleam of approval in Zufar's eyes as she tucked away a good portion of pasta with rich creamy sauce and French bread. When she was done eating, she placed her napkin on the table and attempted to enjoy the view.

'Would you like to go out?' Zufar asked abruptly.

She returned her gaze to him and watched the sunlight dance over his glossy hair. 'Where?' she asked warily.

He shrugged. 'Wherever you please.'

'I thought you'd cancelled all our engagements.'

'I did. But I won't have you cooped up in the suite, climbing the walls. We're not scheduled to fly for another few hours. If you wish to go out, we will.'

She wanted to point out that they were in a fifteen-room suite, hardly a space that evoked a coop. But her eyes lit on the tower again, and she nodded. 'I'd like that. Thank you.'

He rose and held his hand out to her. Pulse jumping into her throat, she placed her hand in his, absorbing the tingles that raced up her arm as she let him help her up from the table.

In their bedroom, he walked her to the dressing room. 'I'll summon your attendants.'

She grimaced. 'Can you not? I'd like to dress myself for once without all the fussing.'

He hesitated, then gave a regal nod before heading for his own dressing room.

The off-shoulder design of the maroon jumpsuit came with wide palazzo pants that made it look like an elegant day dress. The outfit was a little more casual than she'd worn for any occasion during her honeymoon but even before she slipped it on, Niesha knew she would love its easy comfort.

She'd watched Halimah and her attendants closely enough to expertly apply light make-up and twist her hair into a stylish bun in minutes. Deciding on simple diamond earrings, she slipped them on. Then she slid her feet into blood-red heels that matched her belt, scooped up oversized sunglasses and a clutch and left the suite.

As always, Zufar was waiting for her in the living room. He'd swapped his suit for a softer pair of grey trousers coupled with a light blue shirt over which he'd worn a jacket two shades darker than his trousers. His tie was gone, in its place a silk scarf tucked neatly into his collar. Handmade loafers completed his outfit and she stared, thinking he could easily have stepped off a magazine cover. As he drew nearer, she saw the

House of al Khalia monogram embroidered on his jacket pocket. She wanted to say that he didn't need it.

Every inch of him shouted his regal status.

In the lift down, he drew a pair of sunglasses from his pocket and slid them on. The moment they stepped out into the sunny reception, Niesha knew what she wanted to do.

'Can we walk for a while?'

'Not unless you want to be mobbed.' The ever-present paparazzi loitered outside.

She grimaced. 'Then I'd like to just drive around, if you don't mind?'

He nodded. 'It will be as you wish.'

They set off in a smaller convoy.

From the back of the limo, she tried to forget her turmoil and just bask in the sights. But it proved impossible.

Strong hands captured her twisting fingers. 'It will be all right.'

Different words, said by a different voice but both owned by people she knew she was emotionally heavily invested in.

She would never get to meet her mother or hear the real-life version of the sweet words she'd whispered in her ear.

But Zufar was right here, a temptation she'd told herself to resist the moment she'd set eyes on him as a romantic teenager with her head in the clouds. Temptation she knew could decimate her when she took his name and accepted him into her body.

His tempting words were the ones she needed to be wary of because Zufar would never see her as anything other than a replacement for another woman. A woman he hadn't cared about enough to go after. If he'd found it so easy to discard Amira, what hope did she have of ever finding anything deeper with him?

When her feelings grew too much to contain she tried to prise her hands away. He held on tight. 'Tell me what troubles you.'

'I'm scared,' she blurted before she could stop herself. But self-preservation stopped her from expounding.

To her surprise, he nodded. 'I know. You'll recall I, too, have been in your shoes.'

'You've been pregnant?'

He looked startled for a moment, before his mouth curved in a smile. It was the first genuine full smile she'd seen on his face. And it floored Niesha completely.

'No, that is a privilege you will enjoy on your own.'

Smooth.

So smooth, she felt a little of her agitation drift away. And when he meshed his fingers with hers and drew her head onto his shoulder, she went with her insides melting, her heart pounding and her head telling her she was just ten kinds of fool for leaving herself wide open for further heartache.

'Niesha. Wake up.'

The low, deeply voiced command tickled the shell of her ear.

With a small shiver, she blinked awake, and realised she was draped all over Zufar.

She jumped but didn't get very far as the arm clamped around her tightened. She raised her gaze, about to murmur an apology for falling asleep on him, when she noticed where they were. 'We're at the air-port?'

'Yes. You fell asleep in the car. After we drove around Paris for two hours I thought it best to come straight to the airport.'

'I've been asleep for two hours?'

Tawny eyes gleamed at her. 'Clearly you needed the rest.'

The thought that he'd driven around with her even though she'd fallen asleep shouldn't have touched her, not after the stern warning her head had issued her heart.

And yet, she found herself softening against him, the decadent desire to melt into his warmth sucking at her. She told herself she would only give in for a min-ute. Or two.

When his gaze dropped to her mouth, she added one more.

But the kiss she yearned for never came.

Without taking his eyes from her, he gave a casual flick of his wrist, and the door was thrown open, end-ing the private moment that only she had wanted more of, it seemed.

Zufar stepped out, and held out a courteous hand for her.

Niesha placed her hand in his, struggling to reconcile the man who'd driven around the streets of Paris just so she could take a nap with the man who had clearly seen her invitation and declined it.

The baby.

Of course, it was all to do with the baby. How could she have forgotten?

At the first opportunity, she drew her hand from his,

vowing never to repeat her mistake. Besides, with her future in turmoil, the earlier she learned to stand on her own two feet, the better.

She ignored the sharp look he sent her and hurried to board the plane.

For the duration of the flight, she stayed in the bedroom with her tablet for company. By the time they landed in Khalia, she'd devoured everything she could find on her family. And shed a few tears along the way.

Zufar scrutinised her face as they stepped out of the plane but didn't comment. The ride to the palace was also conducted in silence, but when they approached their bedroom, she couldn't hold back any more.

'So what happens now?'

'Once we have irrefutable confirmation, my special council will meet with yours and we'll take it from there.'

It wasn't what she'd wanted to know, but discussing their bedroom arrangements when two kingdoms stood to be plunged into uncertainty felt trivial.

'What do you mean, take it from there?'

He shrugged. 'You will appreciate that this is a unique situation for both of us. We'll need to strategise the best way forwards.'

'You're speaking but not really saying much.'

He dragged a hand through his hair, the first sign that the circumstances they found themselves in weren't straightforward. 'I can't give you an answer I don't have. Not without further investigation.'

'Investigation?' she echoed.

'All signs point to the fact that Rumadah needs its rightful ruler back on the throne. It hasn't had one for two decades.'

'Because a new one couldn't be crowned for twenty-five years,' she added, recalling what she'd read about her country's constitution on the plane. According to the laws, a missing heir to the throne couldn't be ruled out until twenty-five years had passed. In that time a twelve-member council, the same that had served the last King, would rule the kingdom.

In another five years, she would've lost her birthright.

But was it one she wanted, if it meant what she was beginning to fear? Because how could she claim her Rumadian birthright and still remain Queen of Khalia? Zufar's wife?

Her insides shook at the mere thought of walking away from him. It seemed more impossible now than ever. Because the loss of her family wasn't the only reason she'd cried on the plane. She'd also cried because she'd finally accepted that she was in love with Zufar. And painfully accepted that that love would never be reciprocated.

'Perhaps we shouldn't jump the gun just yet. This could all be an elaborate hoax,' she said, more in hope than expectation.

The look in Zufar's eyes told her the same. 'A few days ago I urged you to reconcile yourself to never discovering your past. That landscape has changed and delivered everything you hoped for. Perhaps you should reconcile yourself to this blessing?'

She flinched at the trace of censure in his voice. Before she could respond, he turned from her. 'I need to catch up on a few engagements. Don't wait up for me.'

The last statement was both a blessing and a curse. He intended to find her in their bed when he deigned to return but he didn't care whether she was awake or asleep now that she was pregnant?

Niesha was rubbing at that agonising spot in her chest when the doors opened again and Halimah and the rest of her retinue descended on her.

She forced herself to respond that, yes, she was happy to be back, and that, yes, her honeymoon had been everything she'd dreamed about as they helped her undress and ran a bath for her. She withstood their attention for as long as she could, until she felt as if her face would break if she smiled one more time.

They respectfully retreated when she asked for privacy. With a sigh, she sank into her lavender and jasmine-scented bath. Immediately, a few dozen questions crowded her mind.

Zufar had suggested she be grateful to have her birthright back. But would everyone else feel the same? Would her people even want her once the inevitable announcement was made?

With no definitive answers in hand, she ate a light dinner and went to bed early.

If Zufar came to bed at all, he was gone when she woke, and when Kadira arrived, she was told His Highness had instructed her workload be kept light until further notice.

If he wanted to set tongues wagging about a possible pregnancy, he couldn't have done a better job, she thought with a bite of irritation. All day, Kadira slid smiling, speculative glances at her. And Halimah and her attendants joined in as they helped her prepare for bed.

Again, she didn't see Zufar, even when she woke in the middle of the night.

When she next woke, it was with a heavy, pounding heart.

Today was the day.

Dr Basim had been given forty-eight hours. Whatever happened, she would have a choice to make.

His wife, his Queen, who carried his heir, was herself an heiress to another kingdom. Even though Zufar had known it was inevitable the moment he'd clapped eyes on the pictures of Niesha's parents, he wasn't ashamed to admit a small part of him had hoped that the information would be proved wrong.

Dr Basim and a team of doctors in Rumadah had proved conclusively that Niesha, or Nazira, as she was being addressed in his conference room, was the rightful heiress to the Rumadian throne.

Not that he'd wished for her past to remain a closed chapter to her, but this situation was not at all what he'd anticipated or remotely wanted.

With their reports, however, another bombshell had been dumped into his lap. One that demanded immediate remedy.

He watched the councillors who had accompanied Dr Basim bow and scrape before Niesha. Watched her shy, smiling acknowledgement, and the eagerness with which she absorbed every morsel of information they delivered to her.

For the most part, her seeming return from the dead was very welcome news indeed. And with each moment that passed, he could see the wheels turning in the councillors' minds regarding how to swiftly reclaim their Queen.

A few cast furtive glances towards him, wary of his silence.

The simple truth was that to vocalise his true feelings would've shocked them all. The churning in his chest that had begun long before Niesha's past had been revealed, and which had grown considerably since the revelation, exploded into gut-clenching proportions as he watched them slowly sink their claws into the woman he had claimed for himself.

Or attempted to claim.

Behind his back, his fists curled, his whole body tensed up in battle mode. The thundering of his blood hissed that, regardless of his acceptance of her birthright, he wasn't about to let her go that easily.

You may not have a choice.

He ignored the voice that had been growing louder. By his own bargain, he'd placed an exit clause on their marriage. Whether he chose to accept it or not, a termination date could very well be on its way back to bite him.

He noticed his own councillors sending him questioning looks, but for the first time in his life, he didn't have ready answers available. He hadn't had them back in Paris when the thought had first occurred to him that he might lose Niesha.

'Your Serene Highness, we will need to make an announcement soon. When can we expect you to return to Rumadah?'

This came from the chief councillor, a cunning old man who'd been eyeing Zufar since they entered his conference room.

'Return?' Niesha echoed.

'Of course. Once the announcement is made, your

people will wish to see you, to reassure themselves that you are well.'

'She is well, as you can very well see.' Zufar attempted to modulate his voice, but knew he hadn't succeeded when more eyes turned wary.

'Of course, Your Highness, and we will be grateful to you and to your people for ever for taking such good care of our Queen.'

'But...?' he trailed softly. There was a *but*. It was written on all their faces.

'But...with a thousand pardons, her rightful place is back in Rumadah. Her people need her.'

Simple words.

Heavy, life-altering words, as he very well knew.

Not too long in the recent past his own councillors had pleaded with him in the same manner, urging him to save Khalia after his father's abdication.

Even now, his people needed him. Khalia might have regained her rightful position as a powerful state to be reckoned with but Rumadah had merely trundled along, no one stepping up to make the bold decisions that would take it from a game player to a shot caller.

Without a bold leader to ensure its considerable power was harnessed in the right way, it risked falling into apathy or, worse, into enemy hands. From the research he'd done himself, Zufar knew that the oil-rich country had only stayed on an even course because of its substantial deposits.

A glance around the room of ageing councillors delivered the hard truth that it was only a matter of time before the situation altered for the worse. They needed a true leader, a visionary, who would rule with a firm but compassionate hand.

Someone like Niesha.

His wife.

His Queen.

The mother of his unborn child.

It was impossible.

It was also inevitable that a decision needed to be taken. And soon.

He turned and looked at the two dozen people in the room.

Niesha sat at the head of the table, nodding and making comments where necessary, but he knew her head wasn't in the game. How could it be, when they were all speaking at once?

Over their heads, her gaze snapped up. Wide amethyst eyes met and locked on his, and something deep and profound moved in his chest. *That* sensation had also been escalating, confounding him at the oddest moments.

But far too soon, her gaze dropped away from his as she turned to address the man seated to her right. Whatever he was saying to her wasn't good because after a few minutes she paled a little, even as she nodded.

Enough.

Realising he hadn't vocalised the word, he spoke again. 'Enough.' When he had their attention, he went to Niesha, placed his hand at the back of her chair. 'Give us the room,' he ordered, stamping his tone with implacable authority. 'I wish to speak to my wife in private.'

The councillors looked a little surprised, but one by one they filed out.

'Thank you. I needed a break,' Niesha murmured.

'Then you should've asked for one.' Realising his

voice was still brusque, he modified it. 'This must be overwhelming for you.'

'Despite their collective age, they're like a pack of overzealous wolf pups, all with sharp teeth they don't know can hurt.'

Her description couldn't have been more accurate. He also remembered that pups grew into adulthood, some into alphas who relished a challenge. 'The trick is to train them early, show them who's in charge. Yours doesn't need to be the loudest voice in the room, but it needs to be the final authority.'

The look she gave him was filled with gratitude. As much as he welcomed it, Zufar yearned for another look. One whose absence made the band around his chest tighter by the day.

'I need to write these things down, don't I? To remember them for later.'

'You won't need to. You're their Queen. Leadership was bred into you from birth.' And soon, if her councillors succeeded, she would take it and herself away from him.

She sighed and lifted a hand to rub her temple. A moment later, she straightened her spine, a resolute look settling on her face.

How could he not have spotted signs of her breeding from the moment they met? Royalty was stamped into every fibre of her being, every drop of her blood.

'You wanted to talk to me?'

Words eluded him for a moment as the combination of delicate jaw, sensual mouth and alluring eyes flattened him. But he forced himself to focus. He'd cleared the room to give her breathing space but there was another subject that needed discussing. 'Dr Basim hasn't told them you're pregnant. Is he planning on telling them?'

It would be one way to force her quicker return to Rumadah. A risen-from-the-dead queen would please her people. One expecting a royal heir would be euphoric.

He wondered whether it was a card she intended to play.

She laughed. 'I've barely managed to get their names right.'

Her self-effacing response didn't please him. 'It's customary to keep news of pregnancy under wraps for the first trimester,' he pressed.

She blinked, then rose and went to stand before the floor-to-ceiling windows. Framed against it, she looked almost delicate. But her spine was straight, her resolve absolute. 'I'll tell them when I'm ready.'

Relief and the breath he hadn't realised he held burst through him. She burst it a fraction of a second later.

'Half of the advisers are returning tomorrow. The other half leave on Friday. They want me to accompany them when they return to Rumadah.'

When had these arrangements been made? While he'd been tuned out, feeling sorry for himself? 'Friday is three days away,' he growled. 'We just returned from our honeymoon. I can't leave again so soon.' Especially when he didn't have an answer on how to stop the freight train he could sense heading his way.

Her lashes swept down, veiling her expression. 'I understand. I'm sure I'll be fine on my own,' she said.

That vice threatened to squeeze every last breath out of him. 'I see. And how long will you be gone?'

'Three days. Maybe four.'

The prompt answer froze the blood in his veins. 'Was that the plan all along?'

Her eyelashes lifted. 'I beg your pardon?'

'Use my duty to my people against me?'

She gasped. 'Zufar, I don't know what you're talking—'

He stared down at her, the inevitability of loss continuing to suffocate him. 'And what happens after that?'

Her eyes widen. 'What do you mean?'

'Do you intend to commute back and forth between your kingdom and mine?'

Her forehead gathered in a delicate frown. Then she shrugged. 'This is all new. I don't have the answers, Zufar. But I think you know that I owe it to my people to at least let them know who I am.'

A part of him felt shame for her hurt, but it wasn't enough to overcome the terrible anguish scything its way through him. He despised the feeling. Enough for him to approach her, despite his vow to refrain from touching her.

She had enough on her plate without his ever-growing hunger for her saturating the atmosphere between them. It was a decision he'd made in Prague after watching her sleep, seeing the shadows beneath her eyes, and knowing that he was partly to blame for it.

For the first two weeks of their marriage, he'd never let a night pass without making love to her, his need so great it had confounded him even then. That need had grown into unbearable proportions by the time they'd arrived in Prague.

When the demands of his duties had kept him way from the marriage bed for that first night, he'd watched her for signs that she'd missed him the next morning. There had been none.

The idea that the carnal weakness was on his part alone had brought him up short. And when, night after night, Niesha had made no attempts to reach for him, he'd had his answer. He'd roped her into a bargain to provide him with an heir, but was that all it was for her? Was that the only reason for her welcoming him into her body?

Perhaps that was the reason she could speak so freely of leaving him behind for four days.

'If that's the plan, you'll need to rethink it because it won't be sustainable,' he bit out.

She paled a little, but continued to hold his gaze boldly. 'What are you saying, Zufar?'

'I'm saying that even the shortest of separations has a habit of growing. It's not healthy for any marriage. My parents led separate lives, my mother lived in the east wing and my father lived in the west. Even under the same roof, their marriage was a sham. I do not wish this for myself.'

'I agree, but—'

'I know what I want and it certainly did not involve living in separate countries.'

'So you wish me to renounce my birthright?' she demanded with a hint of tears in her eyes.

Ice gripped his nape hard. 'I'm saying that hard choices need to be made.'

'And you want me to be the one to make them?' Her eyes brimmed, her mouth trembling for one second before she pursed it.

He wanted to lift his hand to her face, brush away her tears, but that would be giving in. For as long as he could remember his father had given in to his mother's every whim, making himself deeply miserable at every turn. Zufar had vowed never to leave himself that vulnerable. But…was it already too late?

'We had an agreement,' he threw at her.

She took in a heavy, shaky breath. 'And I am not reneging on it. I'm only trying to find a way—'

'A way to do what?' He knew he was being unreasonable, but for the life of him, he couldn't stop. He was floundering, hurting her, hurting himself in the process but there didn't seem to be a life raft in sight, and with every moment that passed his anguish strangled him, making him hold tight to the one thing that he knew he couldn't hold onto.

Niesha.

'You promised me five years,' he repeated, as if that would make her fall at his feet, and give him everything he wanted. When really, a greater part of him wanted it to be the other way round. But how could he, without leaving himself desperately exposed?

Slowly her regal head lifted, her eyes condemning him, challenging him to remain obstinate, to keep standing in her way. 'I don't recall signing any piece of paper saying you owned me for five years.'

He wasn't sure why that statement both shocked and made him proud. He had already admitted his flaw in striking that bargain. A part of him applauded her for jumping through that wide loophole.

'I'm aware that all we had was a verbal agreement,' he stated. 'But I still wish you to stand by it.'

Her shoulders sagged a little, but in the next moment she pulled herself back up. 'Don't push me, Zufar. You might not like the consequences.' After a moment, her gaze softened. 'But if you let me work this out on my own, perhaps we can find a solution that works for both of us.'

The only solution he wanted was her here under his roof, in his bed, at his side, bearing his children, loving them the way his mother had never loved him.

'Three days. That's all I ask. Surely you can give me that?'

Could he? Already he felt emptier than he'd ever felt in his life, and she was standing right there in front of him.

Zufar didn't know where he found the strength to nod. 'Of course. Go with my blessing.'

The realisation terrified him that despite everything he'd said he meant it. Because wasn't that something his father would have done? Ripped out his organs if his mother had asked?

'Thank you,' his Queen said, her gaze searching his.

For signs of his obsession, perhaps?

He clenched his jaw, attempting to neutralise his expression. 'You'll let me know of your travel plans once they're finalised?'

She nodded.

He left her in the conference room, calmly walked out even though he wanted to bellow to the skies; to rip himself inside out just so he could reach the pain inside that was decimating him. The walk to his office was the longest he'd ever taken.

Once he was there, he strode to his desk and sank into the chair.

He couldn't even take three days of separation. How would he take a lifetime? Because he knew that was coming too. Unless something changed drastically,

Niesha would be out of his reach even before their child was born.

He slammed his fist on the desk, his thoughts churning a thousand miles an hour. Sunset came and went and still he had no solution. When the door to his office opened without announcement from his private secretary, he nearly snarled.

He managed to bite it back when he saw Malak framed in the doorway.

'I'm hearing all sorts of juicy gossip about you and your new bride, brother,' Malak drawled.

'You know very well what's happening. Your private secretary received the same memo I sent to Galila and Father.'

Malak shrugged as he strolled over to the drinks cabinet and poured two fingers of cognac into crystal glasses. Returning to Zufar's desk, he slid one across the smooth surface. Then he sprawled himself in the chair across the desk.

'I have to say, your new wife is turning out to be quite the surprise, isn't she? I admit, I wasn't very impressed in the beginning, but—'

'Watch yourself, brother,' Zufar warned.

Malak held up one hand as he sipped his drink. 'No disrespect meant, brother. But I'm not the one who harped on about wanting some peace and quiet around here, only to turn around and start tossing dynamite like it was a party favour.'

'Did you come here to make a specific point or are you just here to annoy me? If it's the latter, then bravo, you are succeeding.'

Malak laughed. 'I came to offer you whatever help you need. I may be the selfish playboy the tabloids like to portray me as, but underneath this handsome exterior lives a semi-decent heart that's bleeding for you right now.'

The words were laced with so much amusement, Zufar's irritation mounted. 'You claim you want to help, but all I see is you sitting there drinking my cognac.'

Malak waved a gracious hand. 'Tell me what you need and I will do my best to give you a simple yay or nay.'

Zufar stared into the amber shadows of his drink, two words ticking over and over in his head. *Three days.* He'd agreed to three days. Would she come back? What would he do if she didn't?

'Or I can leave you to brood into your drink?' Malak suggested.

Zufar stood and paced to the window, that feeling of being turned inside out surging to breaking point. He tossed back his drink, then his gaze dropped to the rose garden below his window. He stared at the perfect flowers, his thoughts churning.

After several minutes, his brother joined him, his gaze zeroing in on the same place. 'Why didn't she love us?' Malak asked in a thick, heavy voice.

Zufar was unprepared for the question, just as he was unprepared for the canon of the pain that shot through him. He'd thought he was over that, or at least had suppressed it enough not to feel the agony of his mother's indifference any more.

He shrugged. 'Because she was incapable of it. Ultimately, she couldn't love anyone but herself.' Perhaps it was a flaw he needed to come to terms with, and move on.

Niesha wasn't like that though.

She loved children. She would love their child with the same passion with which she loved his people. The same devotion with which she loved her people enough to threaten to walk away from him and his crown to serve them again. That kind of selflessness was humbling. Inspiring.

How could he stop her from pursuing that, from giving to people who would love her back, and welcome her with open arms the way his people had done?

Malak sighed. 'I wish he'd done something.'

'Who?'

'Father. I wish he'd made a decision one way or the other. Demanded that she love him and us, or leave her. Instead of trailing after her all those years. Instead of making us live each dreadful moment with him.'

'I don't think it was that simple,' Zufar found himself explaining. 'Maybe he was left with very little choice.'

His brother sneered, turned and started walking away. 'Whatever. I'm over it. Anyway, it's been a good talk. If you decide you need me after all, you know where to find me.'

Zufar barely heard him leave. And as he stared into the bottom of his glass, he found his thoughts veering in another direction.

To his father.

CHAPTER TEN

NIESHA STOOD IN front of the plane door, waiting for the attendant to open it. Unlike the flight to Europe, this one had been short and nerve-shredding, her emotions swinging between what awaited her in Rumadah and what she'd left behind.

The last three days had been alternately perfect and horrendous. The coordinated news of her real identity had been greeted with another wave of happy frenzy across the world, the short interview she'd given to explain her unfortunate absence accessed over a billion times online. That had been her public life.

In private, she'd remained in turmoil.

Even though he'd given her his blessing, Zufar had stayed away from her, and in the rare moments when they'd met, his gaze had chilled her. He still came to their bed, but it was only to sleep, with his back to her and a mile between them. When they needed to communicate, they did so via their private secretaries.

That was how she'd found out he'd granted her access to his royal jet to make this trip. That was how she'd found out he'd gone on a whistle-stop tour of his kingdom and wasn't expected back before her departure.

Their conversation in the conference room had left

her bruised and hollow and heart-wrenchingly convinced that her days with Zufar were numbered. It was why she'd thrown herself into this visit.

When he was out of her life, at least she would have this, her new life, to fall back on. The more she'd absorbed about her heritage, the more she was certain she wanted to claim her birthright. Her parents had loved this kingdom and dedicated their lives to it. How could she walk away?

In a way it was easier that Zufar had laid down an ultimatum.

No. It wasn't.

She would have preferred a different ultimatum. One that made loving and dedicating herself to both kingdoms possible. But she knew it was another dream she needed to let go of. Just as she knew she would need to reconcile herself to letting Zufar go.

Divorce.

That was what one of her advisers had cautiously suggested during their meeting in Khalia.

Divorce the man who hadn't meant to be her husband in the first place so she could be free to fully embrace her destiny.

Such an easy suggestion. With such catastrophic consequences for her heart, her soul, every breath she took from here on out.

'We're ready, Your Serene Highness,' the Rumadian attendant said softly, with a blinding smile and shining eyes that hinted of tears. 'And if you'll permit me to say, I'm so happy you're here,' she gushed.

Niesha returned her smile, then her heart lurched wildly as the door slid soundlessly open and sunshine poured into the doorway.

Momentarily blinded, she blinked a few times, smoothing her hands over her royal blue wrap dress before stepping forwards. Immediately, a deafening roar went up over the sound of the still-whirling jet engines.

The lump of emotion wedged firmly in her throat grew as she caught sight of the crowd beyond the barricades set up on either side of the plane.

She paused for one full minute to wave before she slowly descended the stairs.

She'd been briefed on the protocol.

Her council of elders would be the first lined up on either side of the red carpet. Beyond that the senior members of the military…*her* military, would be next in line. Then a few prominent ministers and dignitaries.

So she was startled when a figure broke away from the line and approached the bottom of the steps.

Niesha gasped as the unmistakeable figure of her husband materialised in front of her. 'Zufar…what are you doing here?' she whispered as he stepped forwards and took her hand.

'It is my right as your husband to be at your side, is it not?' he returned.

She kept a smile pinned to her face as he raised her hand and kissed the back of it. Peripherally, she heard the crowd go wild.

'Welcome home, Your Highness,' he intoned deeply.

She took another step down, their height disparity forcing her to look up at him. His face was a perfectly neutral picture of regal discipline, his eyes giving away none of his feelings.

'I don't understand…'

'You don't need to. You're perfectly capable of doing this on your own. But I'm here nevertheless.'

For how long? she wanted to demand. But she'd already broken protocol, albeit through no fault of her own. He took a single step to the side and stood tall and proud and royal, but out of her way.

With a nod, she stepped onto the carpet, widening her smile as the chief adviser held out his hand.

'We are so very fortunate and honoured that you have returned to us, Your Serene Highness. Welcome home.'

All through the greeting of her statesmen and military, she was acutely aware of Zufar's presence one step beside her.

How had he got here before her?

Why was he here?

Was he staying?

The questions tumbled through her mind over the next few hours. At some point it struck her that she'd become an expert at compartmentalising because she managed to talk and walk and respond easily to conversation, even while her insides churned.

But everything fell away the moment they left the State House and approached Nazir Palace, the home she'd lived in so very briefly before losing it all.

Unlike Zufar's hilltop palace, Nazir Palace sat in the centre of the city, right on the doorstep of the people. In fact, hundreds of citizens and tourists were strolling through the public grounds as her motorcade entered the gates and drove through secured gates to the private front door.

Niesha struggled to remember any aspect of her home during the grand tour. Nothing came to mind, not even the toys left in the same position as the day she'd left and never returned. When she said as much, she received sympathetic murmurings.

'You will make new memories, I'm certain, Your Serene Highness,' her chief adviser said with a gentle smile.

Niesha wasn't unaware of the gentle pressure coming her way. Or the way Zufar stiffened each time the subject of her return was casually dropped into conversation.

When they reached her parents' bedroom it all grew too much. 'May I have a moment alone, please?'

'Of course.'

The room emptied immediately, save for Zufar. He walked by her side as she walked through the bedroom suite, touching her father's discarded tiepin, inhaling her mother's silk scarf that still faintly held her scent.

In their dressing room, she picked up her mother's hairbrush, gasping when the faintest memory materialised.

'I remember her…this room. She would sit me on her lap and comb my hair with this brush.' The last of the words dissolved into a sob.

Beside her, Zufar held out his handkerchief.

She took it, her gaze snagging his for a moment. 'Thank you.'

He gave a stiff nod. 'You are strong. You can do this.'

A moment later she was alone. As alone as she'd been from the beginning. As alone as she would be when Zufar left as abruptly as he'd appeared.

You will be all right.

She wanted to laugh. She wanted to cry and scream and throw things. But she bottled it all up because she was a queen. *Twice over.* And queens didn't break down into uncontrollable hysteria.

She reminded herself of that as she gave another interview and expressed her joy to be back home. It came in handy when she danced in Zufar's arms and he held her courteously but stiffly that night at a ball thrown in her honour.

And she reminded herself *many times* of that, the next morning, at the breakfast meeting with her chief adviser.

'As I have said, I will give you an answer in due course once I've given the matter more thought.' She picked up the tea and sipped it, her heart alternately joyful to be sitting in her mother's favourite breakfast chair, drinking from her favourite tea set, and heavy because once again Zufar had made himself scarce the moment they were alone.

'If it is a matter of pride, Your Serene Highness, please be assured it is not necessary. No one will judge you. We are simply thrilled that you are back. But we want you back permanently and as soon as possible. Your kingdom needs you. And the only way to extricate yourself from all things Khalia, we strongly feel, is by divorce.'

Icy water drenched her veins. But a numb part of her had already seen this coming. Wasn't that what Zufar himself had suggested in his own way a few days ago? He'd spoken of hard choices needing to be made. And when it came down to it, wasn't a dissolution of a marriage that was doomed to failure anyway the only option?

'You want me to divorce my husband in order to assume my birthright?'

'At the moment, it seems to be the only course open to us, Your Serene Highness.'

The boulder-sized pain that lodged itself in her chest

made it hard to breathe. The joy of being back among her parents' things faded, her hands trembling as she set her teacup down.

'Very well.' She stopped, those two words birthing a thick sob she had to swallow to keep down. 'I understand—'

She froze as Zufar stepped onto the balcony. The look on his face chilled her to the bone.

'I'm guessing I'm no longer needed here, in that case,' he said, his voice edged with soft deadliness. 'Perhaps you wish for me to make myself scarce?'

'Zufar—'

He batted her words away in that unique way of his. 'You can save your words. I came to say goodbye. You have saved me the tedium of saying a more permanent one at a later date.' His gaze dropped to her stomach before rising to her face again. 'But be assured, Your Highness, that what is mine will remain *mine*.'

The shock of his words rooted her to her chair. Her world turned grey as he executed the perfect military turn and disappeared from view.

From her life.

Another sob threatened to escape. With every cell in her body, she wanted to let it rip free. She contained it as she'd never contained anything else in her life.

She was a *queen*. Queens didn't break.

'Wait! You're what?'

Zufar stared at his brother. 'Which part of it do you need repeated?'

Malak stared at him, shock and apprehension written all over his face. 'All of it. Better yet, let's just pretend everything you said was a joke. I can appreciate the odd joke when—'

'It's not a joke, brother. You said you wanted to help. This is what I need from you.'

Malak snorted. '*Help* means handling a difficult meeting in your stead, or picking out a gift for your wife when you run out of ideas. *Help* doesn't mean tossing your throne in my lap, telling me you're abdicating and expecting me to take your place.'

'Not expecting. Requesting. And the throne is too heavy to toss so you'll just have to settle for sitting on it.'

His brother exhaled noisily. 'I'm glad you're okay with cracking jokes. That means you're not that far gone. That you still have time to—'

'My mind is made up, Malak.' He injected the conviction of his decision into his words.

Once he'd come to the realisation that it was his only option, it had been surprisingly easy. The greater battle of winning his wife's heart was yet to come.

'You really mean it,' Malak observed with a stunned look. At Zufar's nod, he threw out his hands. 'What the hell? I don't want it either.'

'But you will take it because this kingdom is important to both of us. And our people need you too much for you to walk away.'

Malak opened his mouth to protest. But a full minute passed in silence as he breathed in and out, his gaze locked with Zufar's.

Zufar saw the moment duty overcame individualism, when the mantle of responsibility settled firmly on his brother's shoulders. It had been exactly like that for him.

'Okay. I accept.'

He rounded his desk and held out his hand. 'God-speed.'

Malak pulled him into a hug. 'Same to you, brother.'

Five hours later, Zufar stood looking at his father, wondering for the umpteenth time if the visit had been wise. He didn't know. In fact, he wasn't sure about a lot of things any more.

But one thing he saw—and recognised—was the pain of loss on his father's face. It was similar to the one currently clawing deeper roots into his heart.

Was this what it felt like to have something right in front of you and lose it so completely, leaving only a gaping wound?

Because he'd lost Niesha. His foolish attempt to join her in Rumadah to mitigate the looming loss had failed miserably.

'Why have you come here, son?'

Son.

Another wrench of agony joined the endless symphony of pain slashing his heart. Zufar couldn't remember the last time his father had called him that. If ever. Or perhaps he had called him that but Zufar, too wrapped up in his own bitter loneliness, hadn't noticed?

He tried to shake off the feelings but they wouldn't leave him. What else had he missed while he'd been busy feeling wronged and aggrieved? Looking into his father's eyes now, he thought he saw a plea that looked like his own. Even a wry understanding.

As if he saw something Zufar didn't.

For some reason that observation both soothed and terrified him. For so long he'd harshly denounced anything to do with his father. But what if the wrongs he'd condemned his parent for were imprinted in his own DNA after all? What if he'd been predestined to repeat the same sins?

Or…what if they weren't wrong at all? Just an extremely misguided obsession but one that could have been mitigated with the right partner by his father's side?

Again he tried to shake off the disturbing thoughts. They persisted until he realised he hadn't answered his father's question.

'Father, I have some news to share with you.'

Niesha walked into Zufar's library, her heartbeat drumming madly in her ears. She'd come straight from the airport to the palace, the urge to speak to him after an excruciating twenty-four hours without him, paramount.

He was sitting elegantly cross-legged on a large, stripped antique sofa, a book on Khalian history balanced on his knee.

As usual, the sight of him arrested her, slowing her steps as she absorbed his virile essence. He was in one of her favourite rooms of the palace but the books might as well have been candlesticks for all the attention she paid to them.

He looked up, his gaze slowly raking her from head to toe before reconnecting with hers.

'You have returned.' The observation was deep, husky, lethal to her senses.

She gave a jerky nod, then ploughed ahead before she lost her nerve. 'We need to talk.'

He tossed the heavy book to one side and stood. 'I agree,' he said. 'But first I need you to take a look at this.' He picked up a bound document from the coffee table as he came towards her.

She went cold, her heart shredding into smaller pieces. Surely he hadn't drawn up divorce papers that quickly?

'What is it?' Her hands shook as she took the papers he held out to her.

'Take a look,' he commanded softly.

She gathered the nerve to look down at the document. Then her heart dropped to her toes. 'This is… No, it can't be,' she said, although a terrified part of her just *knew*.

'It is exactly as you see, little one,' he murmured.

Niesha gasped, that small endearment she had missed so much momentarily overcoming the momentous, life-changing document she held in her hands.

She searched his face, desperately wanting to know if any of this was a cruel joke that would further pulverise her bleeding heart. But as usual, Zufar's expression was an enigma that challenged and thrilled her at the same time.

But it didn't stay that way for long. As she searched deeper, his eyes grew lighter, his expression clearing to leave ferocious resolution. 'Read the document, Niesha,' he urged again.

Her gaze dropped to the weighty document. At the top of the first page, the heading blared loud and clear—*Petition For Abdication*.

'No,' she breathed again. 'You can't do this.' Her whole body shook as chills went down her spine. 'You can't!' she repeated fiercely.

'I can, and I have,' Zufar replied.

She shook her head. 'No, I won't let you do this.'

He reached forwards and brushed his knuckles down her cheek. 'My fierce Niesha. You cannot change what is already done.'

She flung herself away from him. 'You cannot abdicate. You should've checked with me, Zufar.' Her hand trembled as she waved the paper at him. 'This is unacceptable.'

He merely smiled. 'You will reconcile yourself to this too, *habibti*, because there's no going back.'

'But your people. Your kingdom—'

'Will always be my people and my kingdom. But I will not be their King.'

'Just like that? But why?'

'Because I realised that no amount of power or privilege is worth losing you. My place is with you. By your side. I'd give up a thousand kingdoms for the chance to spend a lifetime beside you.'

Hope flared wide and bright through her heart. 'I…I don't know what to say.'

'Say you're not still considering divorcing me,' he implored, his jaw clenching tight as he waited for her answer.

'Saying that would imply I considered it in the first place.'

The grim smile tugged at his mouth. 'I heard you, Niesha. I'm not ashamed to say it was the worst moment of my life.'

'Then I wish you'd stayed a moment longer because you would've heard me decline the suggestion. I admit it did cross my mind, but only because I thought you wanted it.'

'When did I give you that impression?'

'When you said there were hard choices to be made.

I thought you meant going our separate ways.' Her eyes fell to the paper. 'But you meant this, didn't you?'

He gave a single, solemn nod. 'Yes.'

She swallowed, unable to fully accept the enormity of what he'd done. 'We should've talked about this. Your people will hate me for driving you to this.'

He leaned forwards, brushed his lips over hers. 'They will not. They will throw themselves wholeheartedly at their new King.'

She frowned. 'Their new King?'

He nodded. 'Malak will take my place. The council has already met with him. They're preparing his coronation speech as we speak.'

The progress he'd made without her having any inkling staggered her. She dropped to the sofa, her hand going to her head. 'Zufar...'

He was with her before she'd finished saying his name. He dropped down onto his haunches, his hands settling on her thighs. 'Whether you accept me or not, I will not retake my throne. That is now in my past. I aim to dedicate myself to the future.'

A desperate sob broke free. 'Your future is here with your people.'

'No, my future is with you, by your side, the only position I will accept.'

'But you'll lose everything, Zufar. Your title, your—'

'The only title I wish to assume is that of husband. Lover. Father. If you'll have me.'

'I can't believe—'

'Believe it, little one. For so long I've lived in misery and bitterness. You shone a light into my life where there was only darkness. When I realised my feelings for you had deepened I fought it. I believed, based on

212 SHEIKH'S PREGNANT CINDERELLA

what I'd witnessed from my father, that loving you would make me weak. But I watched you loving everyone you came into contact with, watched them fall under your spell and grow stronger because of it.' He reached for her hand, bringing it up to his lips to kiss her knuckles. 'I'm a stronger person today than I was yesterday and that is because of you. How can I resist craving more of that? More of you?'

'Oh, Zufar, you have no idea how much that means to me.'

'I have a fair idea. I want to be a father to our children. I want to grow old with you.' His jaw tightened for a second. 'But before that I want to strike a new bargain with you.'

'A bargain,' she echoed faintly.

'Yes. If you'll have me, if you'll stay my wife, I promise a lifetime of loving you.'

She gasped, then launched herself at him. His arms immediately folded around her, wrapping her tight against him as she fell off the sofa and into his embrace. She didn't care that they both knelt on the carpet. And she definitely didn't care that she was sobbing.

'Is that a yes?' he demanded, his mouth dropping tiny kisses against hers.

'It's a yes. It's an absolute definite yes. But on one condition.'

He tensed slightly, leaning back to look down into her face. Then he gave one of those very regal nods she adored so much. 'Whatever it is, I agree.'

'Promise me you'll never make such life-altering decisions without discussing it with me first?'

'Niesha, you stepped up to be my Queen when I demanded it. It was my turn to return the favour. Rumadah needs her Queen.'

Her happiness dimmed a little. 'Are you sure, Zufar? Absolutely, irrevocably sure? Is there a cooling-off period for abdication? Can we take it back?'

'Hush, little one,' he said, then dropped a longer kiss on her lips. 'There's no going back. There is only going forwards.' One warm, bold hand splayed on her stomach, gently cradling their baby. 'Besides, this project is going to be a full-time one, I suspect.'

She sighed. 'You will be a great father, Zufar, but I don't want you to be just a father. Our coming together may have been a little unorthodox, but without you I would never have found my family, or claimed my birthright. You've helped me in ways that you can never imagine. I don't want you to give up your life here for me, and I came back to tell you just that—that I'll stay in Khalia and be your Queen if that is the only way to hold onto you. I selfishly want a lifetime with you too. But if you think you'll be happy in Rumadah with me, then I want more for you.'

'It shall be as you wish.'

She shook her head. 'You don't understand. I don't want you to just be my husband. I want you to be my King.'

Shock flared through his eyes. 'Niesha, you don't have to.'

'I want to. Just as you wanted me by your side as your Queen, I want you by mine as my husband and my King. That's another non-negotiable condition.'

A wider smile curved his mouth. 'I get the impression there will be a few conditions along our journey through life.'

'You drove a hard bargain when we met. I learned from the best.'

His hands framed her face, his thumbs caressing her cheekbones as he stared deeply into her eyes. 'Even back then, without knowing why, I knew I couldn't let you go. You were in my heart, in my blood, and I didn't even know it.'

'But you know it now?'

'Without doubt or regret.'

'You're in every fibre of my being too. And I wouldn't want it any other way. I love you, Zufar.'

'And I love and adore you, my magnificent Queen.'

EPILOGUE

'Is Her Serene Highness ready for her next present?'
The words were whispered against her nape, right before
warm kisses rained on her bare skin.

Niesha—or Nazira, as she'd reverted to calling
herself—laughed. 'You can't keep showering me with
gifts, Zufar. One was enough. Twenty is beyond ex-
cessive.'

'I have no idea where you got the impression that I
have twenty gifts for you.'

She chuckled. 'I'm sorry to inform you that your private secretary caved under pressure from mine.'

Zufar's head dropped onto her back and he groaned.

She laughed harder. 'In his defence, I think he has
a crush on her.'

'Well, if my secret is out, then you'll have no choice
but to accept.'

He rolled her over and tugged her into his arms.
Nazira draped herself over his wide chest, deliriously
happy to watch as he reached beneath his pillow, and
brought out a small square box tied with ribbons. It was
the sixth one he'd given her today and it was barely
morning. He'd woken her with deep, intoxicating kissing, and proceeded to take her to heaven and back. As

a start to her twenty-sixth birthday, it had been second to none.

And then the presents had started. That Zufar intended to keep to his promise to deliver twenty presents for all the ones she'd missed was evident.

While she was happy to let him because it pleased him, she was content just counting her blessings.

Just a few short months ago, she'd been drowning in loneliness and despair.

Now, she had regained her past, been crowned a queen and, best of all, was tied for life to the husband of her soul.

She accepted the box, and gasped. The diamond pendant was a replica of her birthmark, the starfish the same size as the mark on her arm. And on the back were the names of her family, etched into the white platinum. 'Oh, it's gorgeous.' Tears brimmed in her eyes as he nudged her upright and fastened the necklace.

'I thought you might want a symbol of how you found yourself,' he murmured. 'And the inscription will keep your family with you, always.'

'Oh, Zufar, just when I think I can't love you any more.'

He drew her back into his arms, then demonstrated that there was another way she could love him more.

After they caught their breath, she reached for the folded piece of paper on her beside table. 'I have something for you, too.' She handed it over and watched him open it.

'This is the guest list for my coronation.'

She held her breath. 'Yes.'

His gaze dropped to the sheet. She knew the moment he spotted the addition. 'You want him there? Are you sure?'

She nodded. 'I reached out to him a few days ago. He responded yesterday with an acceptance.'

Zufar remained silent for a moment and then he nodded. 'If you're happy to have him here, then I will welcome Adir and attempt to put the past behind us.'

She smiled, her heart bursting because she knew it had taken a great effort for him to say that. 'And you're not sore because he stole your intended?' she teased.

'*You* were my intended. The one my heart truly wanted. If Adir is happy with Amira, then I'm happy for them both.'

'I love you, Zufar.'

He kissed her long and deep, until her insides melted. 'Keep saying that to me and I will be your slave in this life and the next.'

They stopped talking for a long time after that.

An hour later, as Zufar watched his wife dress for the start of her birthday celebrations, his breath caught all over again.

He couldn't believe how life-changing loving her had been for him. Gone was the bitterness and misery that had clung to him before he met her. He'd accepted her proposal to make him King mostly to honour her, not because he wanted the position.

For the privilege of loving her and being loved by her in return, he would have happily lived in her shadow for the rest of his life. His acceptance had made her happy.

His upcoming coronation in two weeks wrung happy smiles from her each time she spoke about it. Who was he to deny her any of that? His heart grew to bursting as she dropped the towel on her way to the dressing room and he caught the small swell of her stomach. His cup had truly run over, and he couldn't wait to hold their son in his arms.

He'd foolishly thought he wanted a polished stone to pass off to his people. What he'd been blessed with was a gem that shone brighter than the brightest star in the sky.

For as long as he lived, he vowed to ensure that radiance never dimmed.

* * * * *

If you enjoyed
Sheikh's Pregnant Cinderella
by Maya Blake
look out for the rest of the
Bound to the Desert King series!

Sheikh's Baby of Revenge
by Tara Pammi
Sheikh's Princess of Convenience
by Dani Collins
Sheikh's Secret Love-Child
by Caitlin Crews

Coming soon!

#3657 BILLIONAIRE'S BABY OF REDEMPTION
Rings of Vengeance
by Michelle Smart

When Javier learns his explosive night with Sophie left her pregnant, he's adamant they wed! But warm, compassionate Sophie demands more. Can Javier accept that giving her and the baby his all is the key to his redemption?

#3658 THE ITALIAN'S UNEXPECTED LOVE-CHILD
Secret Heirs of Billionaires
by Miranda Lee

A luxury villa will be the latest jewel in Leonardo's crown, until he discovers Veronica stands to inherit it. Their chemistry is spectacular...but so are the consequences when Veronica reveals she's pregnant!

#3659 CONSEQUENCE OF THE GREEK'S REVENGE
One Night With Consequences
by Trish Morey

Wary of being exploited for her fortune, Athena is devastated to learn Alexios only wants her to avenge himself against her father! But when the consequence of their passion is revealed, he wants her for so much more...

#3660 BOUND BY A ONE-NIGHT VOW
Conveniently Wed!
by Melanie Milburne

Isabella is on a deadline. She has twenty-four hours to wed or she'll lose her inheritance! Andrea knows she can't refuse his proposition for a temporary union. But can Izzy risk surrendering to temptation?

HPCNM0918RA

#3661 SHEIKH'S PRINCESS OF CONVENIENCE
Bound to the Desert King
by Dani Collins

Entertaining Princess Galila at a royal wedding seems frivolous... until she reveals Karim's family's darkest secret. To prevent a scandal, Karim will make Galila his convenient bride!

#3662 THE SPANIARD'S PLEASURABLE VENGEANCE
by Lucy Monroe

Poised to bring the Perez name into disrepute, Miranda must be stopped! But when Basilio meets Miranda, he is captivated. His plan becomes one of seduction...that tests his control to the limit!

#3663 KIDNAPPED FOR HER SECRET SON
by Andie Brock

When Jaco discovers Leah's given birth to his heir, he's determined to shield them from his adoptive family's criminal intentions! He kidnaps Leah and his son, whisking them away to his island...

#3664 THE TYCOON'S ULTIMATE CONQUEST
by Cathy Williams

Arturo is furious when Rose places his latest business deal in jeopardy. Now his greatest asset will be seduction, leaving Rose so overwhelmed with pleasure that she forgets all about the deal. Until he finds himself equally addicted—to her!

YOU CAN FIND MORE INFORMATION ON UPCOMING HARLEQUIN® TITLES, FREE EXCERPTS AND MORE AT WWW.HARLEQUIN.COM.

HPCNM0918RB

Get 4 FREE REWARDS!

We'll send you 2 FREE Books
plus 2 FREE Mystery Gifts.

Harlequin Presents® books feature a sensational and sophisticated world of international romance where sinfully tempting heroes ignite passion.

FREE Value Over $20

YES! Please send me 2 FREE Harlequin Presents® novels and my 2 FREE gifts (gifts are worth about $10 retail). After receiving them, if I don't wish to receive any more books, I can return the shipping statement marked "cancel." If I don't cancel, I will receive 6 brand-new novels every month and be billed just $4.55 each for the regular-print edition or $5.55 each for the larger-print edition in the U.S., or $5.49 each for the regular-print edition or $5.99 each for the larger-print edition in Canada. That's a savings of at least 11% off the cover price! It's quite a bargain! Shipping and handling is just 50¢ per book in the U.S. and 75¢ per book in Canada*. I understand that accepting the 2 free books and gifts places me under no obligation to buy anything. I can always return a shipment and cancel at any time. The free books and gifts are mine to keep no matter what I decide.

Choose one: ☐ **Harlequin Presents®**
Regular-Print
(106/306 HDN GMYX)

☐ **Harlequin Presents®**
Larger-Print
(176/376 HDN GMYX)

Name (please print)

Address   Apt. #

City   State/Province   Zip/Postal Code

Mail to the **Reader Service**:
IN U.S.A.: P.O. Box 1341, Buffalo, NY 14240-8531
IN CANADA: P.O. Box 603, Fort Erie, Ontario L2A 5X3

Want to try two free books from another series? Call 1-800-873-8635 or visit www.ReaderService.com.

*Terms and prices subject to change without notice. Prices do not include applicable taxes. Sales tax applicable in N.Y. Canadian residents will be charged applicable taxes. Offer not valid in Quebec. This offer is limited to one order per household. Books received may not be as shown. Not valid for current subscribers to Harlequin Presents books. All orders subject to approval. Credit or debit balances in a customer's account(s) may be offset by any other outstanding balance owed by or to the customer. Please allow 4 to 6 weeks for delivery. Offer available while quantities last.

Your Privacy—The Reader Service is committed to protecting your privacy. Our Privacy Policy is available online at www.ReaderService.com or upon request from the Reader Service. We make a portion of our mailing list available to reputable third parties that offer products we believe may interest you. If you prefer that we not exchange your name with third parties, or if you wish to clarify or modify your communication preferences, please visit us at www.ReaderService.com/consumerschoice or write to us at Reader Service Preference Service, P.O. Box 9062, Buffalo, NY 14240-9062. Include your complete name and address.

HPI8

SPECIAL EXCERPT FROM

Ⓗ HARLEQUIN

Presents.

*Wary of being exploited for her fortune,
Athena is devastated to learn Alexios only wants her to
avenge himself against her father!
But when the consequence of their passion is
revealed, he wants her for so much more…*

Read on for a sneak preview of
Trish Morey's *next story*
Consequence of the Greek's Revenge.

"Going somewhere, Athena?"

Her breath hitched in her lungs as every nerve receptor in her body screeched in alarm. Alexios!

How did he know she was here?

She wouldn't turn around. She wouldn't look back, forcing herself to keep moving forward, her hand reaching for the door handle and escape, when his hand locked on her arm, a five-fingered manacle, and once again she tasted bile in her throat, reminding her of the day she'd thrown up outside his offices. The bitter taste of it incensed her, spinning her around.

"Let me go!" She tried to stay calm, to keep the rising panic from her voice. Because if he knew she was here, he must surely know why, and she was suddenly, terribly, afraid. His jaw was set, his eyes were unrepentant, and they scanned her now, as if looking for evidence, taking inventory of any changes. There weren't any, not that anyone else might notice, though she'd felt her jeans grow more snug just lately, the beginnings of a baby bump.

"We need to talk."

"No!" She twisted her arm, breaking free. "I've got nothing to say to you," she said, rubbing the place where his hand had been, still scorchingly hot like he had used a searing brand against her skin, rather than just his fingers.

"No?" His eyes flicked up to the brass plate near the door, to the name of the doctor in obstetrics. "You didn't think I might be interested to hear that you're pregnant with my child?"

Don't miss
Consequence of the Greek's Revenge,
available October 2018 wherever
Harlequin Presents® books and ebooks are sold.

www.Harlequin.com